SWORD ART ONLINE

fairy dance

VOLUME 4

Reki Kawahara

abec

bee-pee

YEN ON

NEW YORK

SWORD ART ONLINE 4: Fairy Dance
REKI KAWAHARA

Translation: Stephen Paul

SWORD ART ONLINE
© REKI KAWAHARA 2010
All rights reserved.
First published in Japan in 2010 by
KADOKAWA CORPORATION, Tokyo.
English translation rights arranged with
KADOKAWA CORPORATION, Tokyo,
through Tuttle-Mori Agency, Inc., Tokyo.

English translation © 2015 by Yen Press, LLC

Yen On
1290 Avenue of the Americas, New York, NY 10104
www.YenPress.com

Yen On is an imprint of Yen Press, LLC.
The Yen On name and logo are trademarks of Yen Press, LLC.

The publisher is not responsible for websites (or their contents) that are not owned by the publisher.

First Yen On Edition: April 2015

ISBN: 978-0-316-29643-4

10 9 8 7 6 5

LSC-C

Printed in the United States of America

004

REKI KAWAHARA ABEC BEE-PEE

SWORD ART ONLINE
FAIRY DANCE

SWORD ART ONLINE

"Morning, Sugu. You look sleepy. What were you doing last night?"

Kazuto Kirigaya § The black swordsman who defeated *SAO*, the game of nightmares. His nickname is "Kirito."

"Morning, Big Brother. Ummm...
the internet...and stuff..."

Suguha Kirigaya § Kirito (Kazuto)'s sister. A kendo fighter
in her third year of middle school

"You might be right...
But I have to do it anyway..."

Kirito § The mightiest solo player in *SAO*. In *ALO*, he plays as a spriggan warrior.

"K-Kirito! W-wait...You can't go alone!"

Leafa § A girl who runs across Kirito in *ALO*. She plays a sylph character.

"I'm up here...Yui, Kirito!!"

Asuna § A girl held prisoner in the VRMMO *ALfheim Online*.

"I must say, Kirigaya—oh, pardon me, should I call you Kirito? I really didn't expect you to come all this way. I don't know if that makes you brave or an idiot."

Oberon, the fairy king § The avatar of Nobuyuki Sugou. He has the trust of Asuna's father, and has used it to plot a strategic marriage to Asuna against her will.

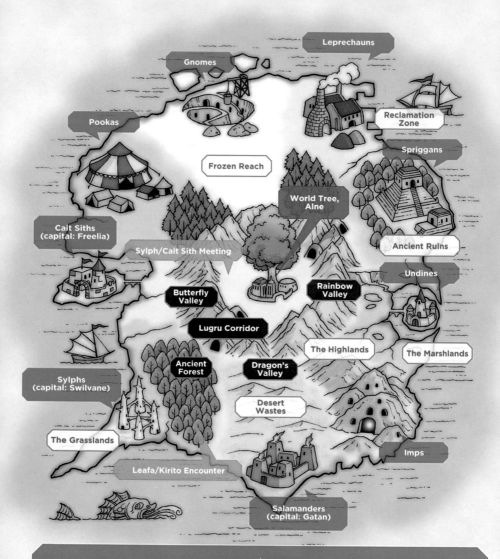

Leprechauns

Gnomes

Reclamation
Zone

Pookas

Spriggans

Frozen Reach

World Tree,
Alne

Cait Siths
(capital: Freelia)

Ancient Ruins

Sylph/Cait Sith Meeting

Undines

Butterfly
Valley

Rainbow
Valley

Lugru Corridor

The Highlands

The Marshlands

Ancient
Forest

Dragon's
Valley

Sylphs
(capital: Swilvane)

Desert
Wastes

The Grasslands

Leafa/Kirito Encounter

Imps

Salamanders
(capital: Gatan)

Alfheim

The setting of the next-gen, flight-heavy MMO
ALfheim Online (ALO), the land of fairies. Alfheim
is divided into nine regions, each of which contains
the capital city of one of the nine fairy races, with
their own unique look and culture.

The nine fairy races are: the sylphs of wind, with
quick flight speed and excellent hearing; the
salamanders of fire, weapon masters with deadly
attacks; the undines of water, skilled at healing
magic and aquatic activity; the gnomes of earth,
hardy miners with good stamina; the catlike
cait siths, nimble animal-tamers; the shadowy
spriggans, masters of illusion and treasure hunting;
the musical pookas, talented singers and musicians,
all; the tinkering leprechauns, skilled at crafting

and smithing; and the imps of darkness, who hold
domain over the caves with their night vision.

Looming over the center of the map is the final
destination of all the players: the titanic World Tree.
At its foot rests Alne, the largest city in Alfheim.

A legendary city in the sky is said to rest atop the
World Tree, and the first race to successfully reach
it and have an audience with Oberon, King of the
Fairies, will be reincarnated as higher beings called
alfs.

As true fairies, alfs will not be subject to the game's
flight limits on altitude and time, making them the
true rulers of the sky.

Map Illustration: Hidemasa Idemitsu

"THIS MIGHT BE A GAME, BUT IT'S NOT SOMETHING YOU PLAY."

—Akihiko Kayaba, *Sword Art Online* programmer

Reki Kawahara

abec

bee-pee

Looking up, one could see a great many lights glimmering in the darkness.

They weren't stars. Hanging from the vast dome above were countless stalactites, glowing faintly from within. In other words, the present location was the floor of a cavern, and the issue was the *scale* of it all.

The span from wall to distant wall was unfathomable. It had to be nearly twenty miles across in real distance. The height of the ceiling was at least five hundred yards, too. And across the floor spread a great many features: cliffs, valleys, lakes frozen white, and snowy peaks—even fortresses and keeps.

Calling it a cave did it no justice. It was an underground room, a subterranean world.

And in truth, it was just that. This world was what spread beneath the fairy land of Alfheim: a singular field of darkness and ice, prowled by terrifying Deviant Gods. Its name—

Jotunheim.

5

"*Bwa-chooey!*"

Leafa the sylph warrior quickly covered her mouth with both hands after the very unladylike sneeze ripped its way free.

She glanced at the entrance to the shrine, imagining one of the enormous Deviant Gods peering inside of it at them, drawn by the sound. Fortunately, the only thing she saw was dancing snowflakes. As they approached the little fire flickering on the floor, the flakes melted away into nothing.

Leafa scrabbled back to the rear wall of the shrine, where she readjusted the collar of her heavy cloak and gave a single heavy sigh. Every time she felt the brief warmth of the little fire, fatigue crept closer, and she had to blink herself awake.

The stone shrine was small; less than fifteen feet in height or width. The walls and ceiling were covered in reliefs of frightening monsters, and the way they seemed to move with every flicker of the light made for a very uneasy atmosphere. But Leafa's companion, sitting with his back against the wall, was nodding peacefully, unaware of and unconcerned with the eerie vibe.

"Hey! Get up!" she hissed, pulling his pointy ear, but he only murmured sleepily. On top of his knee, a tiny pixie was curled into a ball, fast asleep.

"Remember, if you fall asleep, you get logged out!"

She gave his ear another tug. This time, he flopped over on top of her thighs, wriggling in search of a more comfortable position.

With a squeak, she jerked her back straight, and she rapidly clenched and unclenched her hands in midair as she considered just how to strike the guy awake.

Then again, she couldn't blame him for being tired.

The real-time clock in the lower-right corner of her vision told her it was after two in the morning. Leafa was normally fast asleep in her bed at this time of night.

Of course, Jotunheim—and Alfheim above it—were not actual fantasy realms. They were virtual worlds contained entirely within a server somewhere in Tokyo, the capital of Japan, on the planet Earth. Leafa and her partner were engaging in a full-dive simulation through an interface helmet called an AmuSphere.

Leaving this world was actually quite simple. A downward swipe with the first two fingers of her hand would call up a menu window with a log-out button. She could also lie down and fall asleep for real, during which time the machine would sense the change in her brain waves and log her out automatically. When she woke up in the morning, she'd be in her bed back in the real world.

But for right now, there was a reason she had to fight the fatigue that assaulted her. And it was for this reason that she made a fist and brought it down directly onto the spiky black hair of her companion.

The special yellow burst of light that indicated a manual attack was accompanied by a satisfying *crunch*, and her partner leaped up with a yelp. He looked around in a panic, head in his hands— only to see Leafa smiling at him.

"Good morning, Kirito."

"G…good morning."

Her companion was Kirito, a spriggan swordsman with lightly tanned skin and black hair. His rambunctious look—like that of any protagonist from a *shonen* manga—was currently being ruined by the pout on his lips.

"Was I... sleeping?"

"On top of my legs. You should be grateful I only punched you once."

"... I'm sorry. If you want, you could take a nap on mine..."

"No, thank you!" She turned her head to the side and glanced at Kirito out of the corner of her eye. "If you're done being an idiot, maybe you could share the brilliant escape plan you formulated in your dreams."

"In my dream... Oh, yeah. I almost got to that giant pudding à la mode..."

It was stupid of me to expect anything better, she thought, slumping her shoulders. She looked to the shrine entrance again, but the only thing she saw amid the darkness was the flurry of snow dancing on the wind.

Leafa, Kirito, and the sleeping pixie Yui were trapped deep at the bottom of Jotunheim, and they couldn't make their way back to the surface. This was the reason they couldn't just log out.

If they wanted to, they could leave the game at any time. But the shrine was neither an inn nor a safe haven, so if they returned to reality, their avatars would be left behind as soulless husks.

Nothing seemed to draw the presence of monsters like an unattended avatar. Death came swiftly for helpless punching bags, and when they logged in next, they'd find themselves back at their save point: the sylph capital of Swilvane. And then what would their long journey from her character's homeland have been for?

Leafa and Kirito were traveling to Alne, the capital city at the center of Alfheim. They'd left Swilvane earlier today—technically, it was yesterday. They'd flown over vast forests, raced through a long series of mine tunnels, and helped prevent a disastrous attack at the hands of the enemy salamanders, which earned them the gratitude of Lady Sakuya, leader of the sylphs. They'd left her side just after one o'clock.

Excluding bathroom breaks, they'd been in a continuous dive for over eight hours. Alne was still far off in the distance, and they didn't seem likely to reach it any time soon, so the decision was made to call it a night at the nearest inn. They landed in a small village they'd just happened to cross in the midst of the forest.

If she'd only taken the trouble to call up a map, to confirm the name of the village and the presence of any inns. Instead...

"Who would have guessed that the entire village was just a giant monster in camouflage?" Kirito sighed, clearly retracing the same recent memory. She let out a long breath and agreed.

"Tell me about it...Who said there were no monsters on the Alne Plateau?"

"You did."

"I have no recollection."

They both sighed again.

When Leafa and Kirito first landed in the strange village, they were mystified by the lack of any NPC villagers. They had been walking into the largest building they could find, to look for a shopkeeper of some kind, when it happened.

The three buildings that made up the town crumbled simultaneously. They didn't even have time to gasp in amazement at the inn suddenly turning into a slick, shining blob of flesh, as the ground beneath their feet split apart to reveal a dark red cave that squirmed and undulated. What they'd thought was a village was just the mouth of a horrifyingly large wormlike monster, which had evolved to mimic an entire fairy settlement.

It swallowed Leafa, Kirito, and Yui instantly. Leafa was certain that being dissolved in stomach acid would be by far the worst way to die she'd ever experienced in her year of *ALO*.

Fortunately, they didn't meet the earthworm's taste; after a three-minute tour of its entire digestive tract, they were mercifully expelled. Skin crawling from the sticky substance covering her body, Leafa tried to stop her fall with her wings, only to get another shock.

She couldn't fly. No matter how she tried to work the muscles around her shoulder blades to flap her wings, they provided no lift. She and Kirito fell through a featureless darkness and plunged deep into a bank of snow.

After flailing and struggling to work her head out from under the pile of snow, Leafa saw not the moon and twinkling stars of the night sky, but an endless ceiling of stone. A cave—so that was why she couldn't fly. After close scrutiny of her surroundings, she saw a looming, inhuman form slowly prowling across the snows. It was clearly a Deviant God–level monster, something she'd only ever seen in pictures until now.

She quickly leaped to cover Kirito's mouth before he could start shouting. Leafa realized that she had unintentionally made her first-ever trip to Jotunheim, the vast underground realm that was notoriously the most difficult region of *ALO*. Which meant the worm monster wasn't designed to eat adventurers, but force them down into the land of ice.

They stayed still long enough to evade the attention of the five-story-tall creature as it shambled along on its many legs. Once free to move again, they trudged wearily on until they found the little shrine and decided to formulate a plan. Without the ability of flight, however, their options were limited. They'd been sitting along the wall of the shrine, staring at the little campfire for nearly an hour now, without any progress to show for it.

"Well, the problem is I don't know a thing about this Jotunheim place, much less how to escape it…"

Kirito had shaken the sleep out of his eyes. He peered sharply into the darkness outside.

"Didn't the leader of the sylphs say something about this when I handed her all my money? 'You can't make this kind of money without camping out to hunt Deviant Gods in Jotunheim,' or something."

"Yeah, she did," Leafa agreed, traveling back through her memory.

Shortly before they were swallowed by the giant worm, Leafa and Kirito had saved a secret conference between the leaders of the sylphs and cait siths from a deadly ambush at the hands of enemy salamanders. After they did so, Kirito donated a massive sum of yrd to their war chest, at which point Lady Sakuya, leader of the sylphs, had made the previous remark.

"So where *did* you make such a preposterous amount of money, Kirito?"

Leafa's sudden derailment was met with a hum of "ah, um, well…" followed by a muttered answer.

"I, erm, received that money. From a friend who'd played this game obsessively, then decided to retire from it…"

"Hmm."

It was true that when players quit a game for good, they often passed on the cash and loot they'd stockpiled to a friend. That made enough sense to Leafa.

"So, what's on your mind? Something the matter with Sakuya's comment?"

"Well, based on the way she said it, there must be *some* players who do hunt down here, right?"

"There are…apparently."

"Which means there must be other ways to get to and from this place that aren't one-way routes like that worm monster."

She nodded, finally understanding where he was going. "There are…apparently. I've never used them myself, since this is my first time here, but I've heard there's a large dungeon at each of the four cardinal directions in Alne—and at the bottom of each is a staircase leading here, to Jotunheim. They should be…"

She waved a hand to bring up her menu and map. It displayed the large, flat circle that was Jotunheim, but because it was her first trip here, the entire map was grayed out aside from the small area that was their immediate surroundings. She touched the edges of the map—top, bottom, left, and right.

"Here, here, here, and here. Our current location is right between the center and the southwest edge of the map, so the closest staircase would be either west or south. However," she said warily, "the dungeons that house the stairs are guarded by Deviant Gods, as you might expect."

"What're the stats on those things?" he asked airily. She gave him a withering look.

"I know you're tough, but not this tough. From what I hear, a huge party of salamanders attempted to tackle Jotunheim right after it was first opened, and they got easily wiped out by the first Deviant God they faced. Remember how much trouble you had against General Eugene in that duel? Well, he didn't last ten seconds against one."

"...That's saying something..."

"The current strategy requires at least eight people each to be heavily armored tanks, high-firepower damage dealers, and healers for backup. Two light-but-agile fighters are going to be squished like ants against one of them."

"They're formidable, then..."

Leafa glared at Kirito, who, his head bowed like he was nodding in agreement with her, was actually surreptitiously hiding the fact that his nostrils were flared with excitement. She added, "But I'd say it's ninety nine percent likely we'll never make it to one of the exits. Who knows how many Deviant Gods we'll pull along the way, walking from this distance?"

"Really?...Well, I guess on this map we can't just fly over them, huh...?"

"Right. We need sunlight or moonlight to recharge our wings, and that's clearly in short supply in a cave. Apparently, if you play as an Imp, you can fly for a bit underground, though..."

She broke off and examined her wings. The pale green wings that marked Leafa as a sylph and Kirito's gray spriggan ones were both dull and wilted. A fairy that couldn't fly was just a human with pointy ears.

"So that leaves our final option as joining a big raiding party to help get us past those Deviant Gods to the surface..."

"That's right," Leafa agreed, looking outside the shrine.

The only things she could see through the dim, bluish gloom were endless snow, some forests, and an eerie castle looming over it all in the distance. Of course, if they got anywhere near that castle, they'd be greeted most unpleasantly by its monstrous boss and countless underling Deviant Gods. There was no sign of any other players.

"Jotunheim was recently added to the game to serve as the most difficult dungeon yet, for those who weren't getting enough out of the dungeons on the surface. So there're never more than ten parties down here at any time, from what I understand. The possibility that one of them might coincidentally pass right by this shrine is lower than us beating a Deviant God on our own..."

"A test of our real-life luck stat," Kirito smiled weakly. He extended a finger and poked the head of the sleeping pixie on his knee. "Wake up, Yui."

The tiny, pink-clad fairy batted her long eyelashes sleepily, then rose to a sitting position. She covered her mouth with one hand and stretched out the other with a wide yawn. Leafa was entranced by the adorable display.

"*Aawh*... Good morning, Papa, Leafa." Her voice was as delicate and beautiful as the strumming of musical strings.

"Morning, Yui," Kirito responded kindly. "I'm afraid it's actually the middle of the night, and we're underground. Do you think you could run a search to see if there are any players nearby?"

"Yep, sure thing. Just a moment, okay?..." She bobbed her head once and then closed her eyes.

Kirito's little companion Yui was a Navigation Pixie, an in-game helper that anyone could buy for an extra fee. But as far as Leafa knew, Nav Pixies simply read out answers from the help system in a bland autogenerated voice. She'd never seen one with Yui's rich emotional range. In fact, she'd never even heard of a pixie having an individual name and personality.

While she wondered if those things would naturally develop after summoning the same fairy enough times, Leafa waited for Yui's search results.

The pixie's eyes popped open nearly immediately, only to have her ears droop apologetically. She shook her silky black hair back and forth.

"I'm sorry—there were no player signals within the range of my data search ability. In fact, if I had been paying close enough attention to spot that the village was not marked on my map..."

Leafa felt compelled to reach out and stroke Yui's hair, as the little fairy hung her head sadly.

"It's not your fault, Yui. I kept you busy by asking you to keep an eye out for other players. You can't blame yourself for this."

"...Thank you, Leafa."

As Leafa looked into those teary eyes, she couldn't bring herself to believe that it was just a piece of program code. She put on her most heartfelt smile and stroked Yui's tiny cheek before turning to Kirito.

"Well, at this point, I suppose it can't be helped. We've just got to do what we can."

"Do...what exactly?" Kirito blinked. This time, Leafa gave him a confident grin.

"See if we can make it to one of those staircases and up to the surface on our own. The only thing we accomplish by sitting here is wasting time."

"B-but you said it was impossible..."

"I said it was ninety nine percent impossible. Let's bet on that remaining one percent. If we pay close attention to the movement patterns and eyelines of the wandering Gods, we might just make it."

"You're so cool, Leafa!" Yui piped up, applauding. Leafa threw her a wink and got to her feet. But Kirito grabbed her sleeve and pulled her back down.

"Wh-what?"

She awkwardly fell on her bottom and was about to launch a protest when she saw those black eyes staring into her at close range. He had fixed her with a fierce glare, and his voice lost its earlier frivolity.

"No...I want you to log out. I'll watch your avatar until it's gone."

"Huh? Wh-why?"

"It's almost two thirty now. Aren't you a student? You've been in a dive with me for eight hours already today. I can't force you to spend any more of your time here."

"..."

Leafa had no response to this sudden demand. Kirito continued.

"We don't even know how long it will take to walk there in a straight line. Evading the search radius of those gigantic monsters could double the travel time. Even if we reach the staircase, it'll be morning by then. I need to get to Alne at all costs, but it's a weekday for you. I think you should log off."

"I...I'm fine, I can handle one measly all-nighter," she protested weakly, trying to put on a brave face.

But Kirito released her sleeve and bowed his head formally, attempting to force the conversation to a close.

"Thank you for everything, Leafa. It would have taken me days and days just to gather basic information about this world without you. It was only because of you that I could get this far in only half a day. I can never thank you enough."

"..."

Leafa clutched her hands together, unable to bear the sudden pain that stung her breast. She didn't know why she was hurting. But her lips moved automatically, pushing the trembling words out.

"...I didn't do it just for you."

"Huh...?"

Kirito raised his head, but Leafa firmly looked away, her voice hard.

"I came this far...because I wanted to. I thought you understood that. What do you mean, 'force me to spend my time with you'? Did you think I was doing all of this against my will?"

The AmuSphere detected the emotions rising to the front of her mind, and translated them faithfully into teardrops welling in her eyes. She blinked furiously to stifle them. Yui looked at each of them with panic, and Leafa had to stand and face the exit to avoid her gaze.

"Today's adventure was the most fun I've had since I started playing *ALO*. There was so much excitement and drama. Finally, finally, I was able to believe this world was another reality of its own, but now…"

She vigorously rubbed her eyes with her right arm and turned to run out into the darkness.

But before she could—

An alarming, bizarre sound, neither thunder nor tremor, sounded from very close by.

Brrroooo! It was a howl from the throat of an extremely large monster, no doubt about it. It was followed by thudding, ground-shaking footsteps.

Oh no, I just had to shout and draw a Deviant God down on us! I'm so stupid, stupid, stupid, she thought to herself. But if there was one way to make up for her mistake, it was that she could run out into the open and draw the beast away.

Before she could move, Kirito was behind her, holding her arm back.

"Let me go! I'm going to pull the monster away so you can keep going," she hissed, but he cut her off with a sharp glance.

"No, wait. Something's wrong."

"Wrong? What…?"

"It's not one of them."

She stopped to focus her ears—he was right. Aside from the low engine rumble of the Deviant God's roar, there was a whistling sound, like wind through branches. Leafa held her breath and tried to shake his hand off her arm.

"If there are two of them, that makes it even more imperative! If either of them targets you, it's all the way back to Swilvane to start over!"

"It's not that, Leafa!" exclaimed Yui from Kirito's shoulder. "The two approaching Deviant God monsters…are attacking each other!"

"Huh?"

Leafa blinked in surprise and listened again. Indeed, the rumbling footsteps were not the steady gallop of creatures approaching on a run, but the uneven pattern of two beasts circling each other.

"B-but…why would two mobs be fighting each other…?" she muttered in shock, her crushing sadness instantly forgotten. Kirito seemed to have made up his mind.

"Let's go out and see. This shrine isn't much of a shelter, anyway."

"G-good idea…"

Leafa joined Kirito and snuck out into the swirling snows and darkness, her hand on her katana hilt.

It only took a few steps for them to spot the Deviant Gods that were the source of the cacophony. The pair of monsters slowly approached from the east, like two small moving mountains. They were at least seventy feet tall, by any estimate. Both were the bluish-gray color unique to all Deviant Gods.

There was a slight difference in size between the two: The one that rumbled like an engine was larger than the one that whistled like the wind.

The bigger one might charitably have been described as humanoid. It was a giant with three faces stacked vertically, and four arms sprouting from its sides. Each of the faces was sputtering individually, stony and menacing like evil deities, and the combination of their muttering created that odd engine rumbling. The four arms each held a titanic sword, as crude and blocky as steel rebar from a construction site.

The smaller Deviant God was absolutely incomprehensible in design. The large ears and wide mouth were vaguely elephantine, but the body was flattened and round like a dumpling, supported by around twenty clawed legs. It was like a jellyfish with the head of an elephant. It reared up in an attempt to slash at the three-faced giant, but the whirlwind of those swords kept the creature from reaching its target. Each time the tip of one of the swords hit the dumpling body, filthy black liquid sprayed out like mist.

"Wh…what's going on…?" Leafa wondered in amazement, all thoughts of hiding forgotten.

There were three basic scenarios in which monsters in ALO might fight one another.

The first was if one of the monsters was a pet that had been tamed by a cait sith player, who were known for their taming skill. The second was if a pooka charmed one with their characteristic battle songs. The third was if they'd been confused by illusion magic.

But none of those applied to this battle. A pet could be instantly identified by its light green cursor, but both Deviant Gods' were the standard-monster yellow. There was no music, only rumbling, whistling, and shuffling footsteps. Nor was there any hint of the visual effects of illusion magic.

The two monstrous creatures continued their battle without a thought spared for their flabbergasted audience. After a few moments, it became apparent that the three-faced giant's superiority over the jellyphant was decisive. One of its swords caught a clawed tentacle at the base. The appendage flew free and landed close enough to send vibrations through Leafa's body.

"Um, do you think it's dangerous to stand here?" Kirito wondered. Leafa agreed, but she was frozen still. She couldn't take her eyes off the elephantine Deviant God, whose wounds were spurting black blood over the white snow.

The maimed god gave a whirling screech and attempted to disengage again. But the giant had other plans; it leaped onto the dumpling body and swung its blades with wild abandon. The jellyphant was pushed into the ground by the pressure, its cries growing weaker and weaker. Countless ugly gashes were struck into its gray hide, but the giant above showed no mercy.

"Let's help it, Kirito," Leafa said. If she was shocked by this sudden thought, Kirito was three times as flabbergasted. He looked back and forth between Leafa and the giants.

"Wh-which one?"

He had a point. The three-faced one seemed at least somewhat familiar with its humanoid shape, while the jellyphant was just plain horrifying. But the choice was clear.

"The one being picked on, of course," she answered. Kirito's next question was predictably sensible.

"H-how?"

"Umm..."

She had no response to that one—Leafa had no idea how to help it. But even as they stood there, the giant was slicing deep furrows in the grayish hide of the elephantine creature's back.

"...Just do something, Kirito!!" she wailed, clutching her hands together. The spriggan boy looked upward in frustration and ran his hands through his black hair.

"But I don't know what that something should be..."

Suddenly, he stopped moving and gave the beasts a hard stare. His eyes narrowed, light flashing deep within them. She could practically see the high-speed thoughts racing through his brain.

"If there's a meaning behind that body type..." he murmured to himself. Then he looked around with a start and whispered to the tiny pixie on his shoulder, "Yui, is there any water nearby? Lake or river, anything will do!"

She blinked in surprise, but answered him without question. "There is, Papa! There's a frozen lake about two hundred yards north of us!"

"Good... Ready, Leafa? We're going to run there like our lives depend on it."

"Um...huh?"

When he spoke of body type, was he referring to the three-faced, four-armed giant? What did that have to do with a water surface?

Kirito pushed her lightly on the back and pulled something from his belt that looked like a thick nail. Leafa suspected it was a throwing pick, but she'd never seen anyone use them before. With all the powerful long-range magic in ALO, it was nearly pointless to spend time training up the Throwing Weapons skill.

But with a practiced motion, Kirito spun the five-inch pick within his fingertips and raised it above his shoulder.

"Yah!"

He flicked his hand forward faster than the eye could follow, and the metal nail shot forth in a blue line.

It struck the giant's top face right between its gleaming, dark red eyes.

To her surprise, Leafa noticed that the massive creature's HP bar actually went down a single pixel. He couldn't possibly break through that Deviant God's powerful armor with such a toylike implement unless his skill level was incredibly high.

It was only a tiny drop in the bucket of the giant's massive store of HP; the real takeaway was that any damage had been done at all. Because now...

"*Bbbrrrooo!*"

It roared and turned three pairs of eyes from its previous victim to its new target: Kirito and Leafa.

"Time to run!" Kirito screamed and turned north, spraying snow as he dashed.

H-hey... Leafa mouthed in surprise, then took off after the rapidly shrinking spriggan. A moment later, the ground beneath her feet rumbled and her ears were filled with the sound of bellowing. The giant was chasing them.

"W-wait...Aaaaah!"

Leafa was now running as fast as her legs would go, but Kirito was pulling even farther away, his form as perfect as an Olympic sprinter's. She'd experienced his running speed before in the Lugru Corridor on the surface world above, but it wasn't quite so thrilling when he was using it to leave her in the dust.

"Thiiiiis suuuuuucks!" she wailed, as the massive thudding footsteps drew closer behind her. The Deviant God was thirteen times Leafa's height, so the ground it covered in a single step must be about the same. She could practically imagine those giant rebar swords swinging at her back, and put every ounce of her strength—technically, every ounce of her brain's commands—into running after Kirito.

Suddenly the figure in black skidded to a halt in front of her with a spray of snow. Arms open wide, Kirito spun around to catch her. Despite the situation, she couldn't help but feel a little flushed in the face, and turned to look back.

The three-faced giant loomed over them, terrifyingly close. A few more steps and it would be upon them. Just a single blow from its massive swords would easily obliterate lightly armored fighters like Kirito and Leafa.

What in the world is your plan?! she silently hissed at her partner. At nearly the same moment, a monstrous cracking sound echoed throughout the underground clearing.

The giant's enormous, tree-trunk leg had punctured the ice hidden beneath the snow drifts. Kirito had stopped them directly in the center of the snow-covered lake.

The ground just fifty feet ahead of them cratered in, revealing dark, clear water. The three-faced giant plunged into the hole of its own creation, sending up a towering plume of water.

"P-please, please just sink..." Leafa prayed with all of her being, but it would not be that simple. Almost immediately, a face and a half emerged from the water and began sloshing toward them. It must have been using the pair of arms below the surface like oars, and, despite its rocklike exterior, it indeed proved itself a skilled swimmer. If dropping the beast into the lake was Kirito's plan, then the gamble had backfired.

She tensed herself for another mad dash, but Kirito held her close and did not budge. His grip was so tight, the game's anti-harassment code could have kicked in at any moment. He stared down the approaching giant.

"...Uh...y-you don't mean to..."

Does he just want to die here? she wondered instinctually.

Not long ago, she'd suggested that they allow themselves to be killed so that they could respawn at their save point: Swilvane, capital of sylph territory.

That was not an option. Every event, every incident that had occurred throughout this long, long day had told her how urgent it was for Kirito to get to the World Tree looming over Alne in the center of the map. The spriggan boy dove into ALO solely to meet someone atop it. They'd overcome all these challenges just for that purpose.

"No, you can't—! You have to…" She struggled to free herself from his arms, but her piteous wail was interrupted by another large splash.

Leafa turned her head with a start to see a fresh plume of water behind the approaching three-faced giant. Its whirling, high-pitched roar was that of the elephant-headed Deviant God the giant had been tormenting just moments ago. All this work to pull the attacker away, and it had followed after them.

And as Leafa watched in shock and awe, all other details forgotten, it burst through the surface of the water, stretching out its grasping limbs, nearly twenty in all, and clung to the giant's faces and arms.

Baroomf! the giant grunted in rage, attempting to swing its heavy iron swords. But the water slowed its movements, and the jellyphant's grip stayed strong.

"Oh…I see," Leafa murmured in wonder.

The jellyphant was an aquatic monster by nature. On land, the majority of its many limbs had to be used to support its dumpling body, but now its bulk was floating on the water's surface, leaving all of those legs free to attack. Meanwhile, the giant had to use two of its arms to paddle, halving its combat ability.

When Kirito was muttering about body type, he'd been referring to the elephantine Deviant God. In retrospect, it seemed perfectly obvious to question why a creature modeled after a jellyfish would be on land. Leafa felt a twinge of disappointment in herself.

Like a fish—well, a jellyfish—taking to water, the wiggler climbed atop the three-faced giant, pushing it down beneath the surface. The water swelled now and then with the struggle of the massive creatures, hitting the lip of the ice to spray through the air.

Suddenly, the jellyphant screeched louder than usual, and its body flashed brightly. The light turned to fine sparks, which shot through its twenty legs and into the water.

"Oh…"

"Yes!!"

Leafa and Kirito exclaimed together. The three-faced giant's HP bar was quickly plummeting. Leafa used her Identification skill, which displayed a number with six digits trailing downward with every burst of sparks.

There was a series of red flashes beneath the surface that caused several jets of steam to erupt—possibly the three-faced giant's final struggle—but it had little effect on the jellyphant's health. Eventually, the rumbling roar slowed down and died away. In the next moment, a mammoth explosion of tiny polygonal shards obscured Leafa's vision.

She turned away for a moment, and when she looked back, there was only one cursor left.

Hrroooooo, the jellyphant exclaimed in victory, raising its many appendages into the air before proceeding to swim through the lake.

It hoisted itself onto the shore, great waterfalls running off its massive bulk, and began to cross the creaking ice toward them. Leafa watched with apprehension.

The creature's footfalls shook the ice beneath them as it approached. When it stopped before them, she marveled again at the preposterous size of the thing. Those tentacles, seemingly so thin and fragile when it was fighting the giant, were too large for her to fit both arms around up close. They stretched high like tree trunks, supporting the dumpling-shaped body that was only vaguely visible far overhead.

The face at the front of its wide trunk really did look a lot like an elephant's. The flappers that were actually more like gills than ears spread to the sides of the round face, and the drooping mouth hung almost as low as those pendulous limbs. It had three gleaming eyes covered in black lenses on either side of the face, which would have been creepier if it weren't for their humorous triangle shape, which made them look like rice balls.

"So...what do we do now?" Kirito wondered.

It was Leafa's idea to save the elephant creature, but she hadn't spared a thought for what would come after that. It was still a terrifying Deviant God standing before them, its cursor a hostile yellow. One swipe of its clawed limbs would easily kill the both of them.

But the fact that it had approached so close and still hadn't attacked them proved that this was already an irregular scenario. In a high-level hunting ground like Jotunheim, common sense said that every monster would fly into a rage and attack any player that crossed its field of vision. The fact that it was not doing so gave Leafa hope that it would leave them alone and eventually shuffle away...

A second later, her hopes were dashed. It whistled and extended its long nose straight at them.

"Ugh..."

Kirito prepared to leap out of the way, but Yui pulled on his ear with an adorably tiny hand. "It's all right, Papa. The little one's not angry."

Little one? Leafa's jaw nearly dropped at the irony. Suddenly, the finely separated tip of its nose snaked around the both of them and lifted them straight off the ground.

"Hyeeek!" Kirito wailed pathetically. Leafa couldn't even manage a squeak. The elephant head easily lifted them a few dozen yards into the air and tossed them not into its mouth, but onto its back. Fortunately.

They landed butt first, bounced, and fell again. The jellyphant's body had seemed slick from a distance, but it was actually covered in thick, short gray hairs. Once Kirito and Leafa were safely settled in the center of its back, it roared again—apparently in satisfaction—and began moving about as though nothing had happened.

"..."

After sharing a wordless glance with Kirito, Leafa gave up attempting to understand what was happening and stared out at their surroundings.

Being the "land of eternal darkness" did not mean that Jotunheim was actually pitch-black. The stalactites clinging to the ceiling gave off a faint glow, which glimmered dimly off the snow coating the ground. If the place weren't so deadly, it would have been quite beautiful. The dark forests, the jutting cliffs, and the towers and castle looming over it all were easily visible from their present vantage point.

After a minute of riding on the back of the jellyphant and feeling the vibrations of its twenty legs, Kirito murmured, "Do you suppose... this is the start of some kind of quest?"

"Umm..." Leafa wondered for a moment. "If it was a quest, we would have gotten some kind of prompt or start log by now."

She waved a hand to indicate the upper-left area of her view. "Since there was nothing like that, it'd probably be more of an in-game event than a simple commission quest with an obvious beginning and end. But that's a troubling sign..."

"Why is that?"

"If it's a quest, we're guaranteed to get some kind of reward at the end. But since in-game events are more like a little prefab drama involving the players, we can't be assured of a happy ending."

"Meaning... we might be heading for something unspeakably awful?"

"Very possible. I made the wrong choice in a horror-themed event once and got boiled to death in a witch's cauldron."

"Wow. That's messed up," Kirito said, his smile looking more like a grimace. He brushed the heavy hair at his side. "Well, we can't put this horse back in the stable. Er, this jellyphant? And we'd probably take tons of damage jumping off from this height, so I guess we just ride it and see what happens? Um... I know it's a bit silly to bring this up now, but..."

"What is it?"

The spriggan looked at Leafa, his expression serious again, then dipped his head.

"I'm sorry about what I said earlier, Leafa. I made light of your feelings. Maybe I wasn't taking this world seriously enough. 'It's just a game,' I told myself. But I should have known already that whether the surroundings are real or virtual, the things you feel and think *are* real, and the truth…"

A look of anguish crossed his downturned face. For an instant, Leafa felt she saw something familiar in that expression, but she put the thought aside and waved her hands in supplication.

"N-no, it's my fault. I'm sorry…After all you did to help me and the rest of the sylphs, I should know perfectly well that you don't see *ALO* as just another game."

Lately, Leafa had come to feel strongly that there was something about this new VRMMORPG genre that tested each of its players.

Generally speaking, it was a player's pride that was being challenged. This was a game, so it was impossible to win all the time. You might fall into a trap set by players of an enemy race. You might get into a fight and simply be beaten into the mud.

When that happened, how hard could you struggle? If you lost, how would you regroup and hold your head high? That was the test. In traditional video games played on a flat monitor, there was no expression of emotion unless you entered a specific command. If you lost, the most that happened was a frowning emoticon in the chat window. But in the full-dive environment, every player's emotions were written plainly across his or her face. You might even be seen shedding tears of frustration.

Many players glibly abandoned a disadvantageous fight or logged out the moment they lost, specifically in order to avoid showing anyone that kind of emotion. Leafa, too, wanted no one to see her cry, if she could help it.

But the mysterious spriggan before her seemed to spare no thought for the concept of maintaining face. When they were ambushed by the salamanders in the Lugru Corridor and when he was being pulverized by General Eugene's legendary sword, Kirito made no attempt to hide his anger and frustration—he struggled and scrabbled until he ultimately emerged victorious. No one who wrote this off as "just a game" could do such a thing.

"Can I…ask you something?"

What game did you play before this? What are you like in real life? Leafa nearly asked, but she bit her lip. It wasn't right to ask other VRMMO players about their real lives and identities unless you were very close.

She shook her head and told Kirito not to mind, grinning. "I guess this means we've made up. I can stay up as late as it takes. I'm at the time of year where I don't have to go to school if I choose not to."

Leafa extended her right hand. Kirito chuckled and squeezed it. She started shaking it vigorously to hide her embarrassment, but only got more self-conscious when she noticed Yui grinning happily at the two of them. She let go and turned away, certain that her face must have gone red to the tips of her pointy ears.

The elephantine Deviant God continued trundling on, totally unconcerned with the conversation taking place on its back. When she looked to the direction of their travel, Leafa's brows knitted, her blush completely forgotten.

"What's wrong?" Kirito asked. She reached out and pointed ahead.

"We were supposed to be heading for the staircase either to the west or the south, right? I think it's taking us the exact opposite direction...Look."

She was pointing through the darkness to a vast silhouette taking shape ahead. It was an upside-down conical structure dangling from the gently curved ceiling of Jotunheim. An endless series of tiny branches draping down came together to form a kind of net, woven around an impossibly massive pillar of ice.

The distance-blur effect of the game's visual engine told her that it was at least five miles away, but it was so large that it seemed closer than that. A number of blinking lights were embedded in the icicle, and their steady flickering pattern lent the structure an awesome grace.

"What's all that twisty stuff around the giant icicle?"

"I've only ever seen that in screenshots...They're the roots of the World Tree."

"Huh...?"

She cast a sidelong glance at Kirito's squinting face before continuing. "See, the roots of the tree go so far into the earth of Alfheim that they hang down from the ceiling of Jotunheim. Our friend here isn't taking us to the outer rim of the cave, he's heading for the center."

"Hmm...Well, since the World Tree *is* our final destination, is there any way we can climb those roots up to the surface?"

"I've never heard of anything like that. Besides, look at them. Even the lowest-hanging tendril only comes halfway down to the floor. That's got to be hundreds of feet tall, and there's no flight down here. We can't get up there."

"I see," Kirito sighed, then switched gears with a grin. "Then we just have to trust our weevil, or isopod, or whatever he is. We don't even know if he's escorting us to a feast at the palace, or if *we are* the feast."

"W-wait. Iso-what now? If anything, it's an elephant or a jellyfish monster," Leafa instructed him, but Kirito raised his eyebrows in surprise.

"What, you don't know about giant isopods? They're on the bottom of the ocean, like pill bugs that are this big..." He stretched out his hands to a terrifying size. Leafa shivered and quickly cut him off.

"Okay, I get the picture! Let's just give him a name, then. A cute one!"

She looked at the furry, dumpling-shaped body—and the round head nearly hidden at the other end—and tried to think of something with *zo* in it, which was the word for "elephant." *Yuzo*? No...*Zoringen*? Not that...

"How about Tonky?" Kirito piped up suddenly. Leafa blinked in surprise. It was certainly cute enough, but where did he get that name? Hang on...something about "Tonky the Elephant" sounded familiar.

After two seconds of trawling her memory bank, the answer came to her. It was the name of an elephant in a picture book she'd had as a child. As the story went, after a massive war, zoos were ordered to put down their wild animals. The heartbroken trainers gave the animals poisoned feed, but clever Tonky the Elephant didn't eat it. Instead, he kept rearing up on his hind legs until he eventually starved to death. Leafa remembered bawling her eyes out when her mother had read the story to her.

"Kind of seems like an ominous name to give it," she muttered, and Kirito grimaced.

"Good point. It was just the first thing that popped into my head."

"So you know that story, too, huh? Well, fine. Let's go with that!" Leafa thumped her fist into her palm and stroked the fur at her feet. "All right, Deviant God. From now on, your name is Tonky!"

The creature gave no response, of course. She chose to interpret that as a lack of disagreement. If it was turned into a pet through the use of the Taming skill, the name could be made official within the game, but she'd never heard of even the master tamers of the cait sith succeeding in bringing a Deviant God to heel.

From atop Kirito's shoulder, Yui waved her tiny hands at the creature, which was many hundreds of times larger than she. "It's nice to meet you, Mr. Tonky! Let's be good friends, okay?"

This time, they saw the floppy ear/gill at the side of the creature's head wave slightly, perhaps it was just coincidence.

The jellyphant named Tonky continued northward along the bank of a frozen river. On the way, they had more than a few encounters with other wandering Deviant Gods trudging through the wastes. But for some reason, the creatures only threw the group a glance from beyond the trees or hills that separated them, and walked on without further interest.

Perhaps they saw Leafa's party as nothing more than an accessory of Tonky's, but that didn't explain why the three-faced giant had attacked the beast. The only potential reason that came to mind was that all the Deviant Gods they passed without incident were nonhumanoid in shape, like Tonky itself.

She turned to Kirito to ask his opinion and was aghast to see that once again, the spriggan was fast asleep, his head lolling. She clenched her fist, ready to pound him, when she was struck with a much better idea and began shoveling up the snow that had accumulated on Tonky's back.

Before the snow could dissipate, she quickly tugged on the back of Kirito's collar and dumped it down his back.

"*Hweeg!!*"

Kirito leaped up with a strangled yelp as the chilly sensation hit his back. She bid him good morning and asked the question that had been on her mind a moment earlier. The spriggan sulked for a bit, then pondered the idea.

"So you're suggesting...within the Deviant Gods, there are fights between the humanoid kind and the animal kind?"

"Perhaps. Maybe the humanoid ones would only attack Tonky's kind."

The Jotunheim zone had only been added to the game a month ago during a major update, and it was so difficult that very little progress had been made on it. If this situation represented some kind of special event, it was quite possible that Leafa and Kirito were the first players in the entire game to realize it. If a Deviant God hunting party had witnessed the battle between Tonky and the giant, they would have merely waited for Tonky to die before finishing off the other one.

"Well, only Tonky and the designer of this event know the whole truth. Let's see how this plays out," Kirito said, rolling onto his back. He put his hands behind his head and crossed his legs at the knee. Yui flitted off of his shoulder and landed on his chest, then assumed the exact same position as him. Irritated by this lack of caution and making a mental note to hit him with a freezing spell the next time he fell asleep, Leafa looked at the time readout in the corner of her vision. The pale digital numbers said that it was already past three o'clock in the morning.

Leafa had never stayed logged in after two at the latest, so this was uncharted territory for her. She brushed the thick fur at her feet, feeling conflicted over her very first all-nighter in a video game.

The odd Deviant God continued at its steady pace, completely unconcerned with its tiny passengers. It finally stopped at the top of a gentle hill that was covered in snow and ice.

"Wow…"

Leafa walked up closer to Tonky's head and marveled at the sight before her.

It was a hole. But the word *hole* wasn't adequate to describe the scale of the thing. It was a vertical shaft so wide across, the far side was hazy with distance. The sharp, sheer cliffs were covered in a layer of thick ice, too. That ice was transparent white near the top, but gradiated as it descended into the depths, first to blue, then to deep indigo, then finally to pitch-black. No matter how hard she squinted, there was nothing but darkness down there.

"Wonder what'd happen if we fell," Kirito muttered nervously. Yui gave him a perfectly serious answer.

"According to the map data I can access, there is no defined floor to the shaft."

"Gnarly! So it really is a bottomless pit."

Both Leafa and Kirito inched backward and headed for the high ground on Tonky's back. But before they could get there, the Deviant God's body shifted into motion.

It's not going to toss us in there, is it? she thought frantically, but the creature, thankfully, did not seem to be so ungrateful. It folded its twenty legs inward, lowering its massive bulk to the ground in one even movement.

After several seconds, the bottom of Tonky's trunk thudded heavily on the snow. It gave a brief wheeze, tucked the elephantine trunk underneath its body, and finally stopped moving altogether.

"…"

They looked at each other, then carefully descended off the creature's back. A few steps away, they turned back to find that it was neither elephant nor jellyfish anymore. With its tentacles and head firmly tucked beneath its body, the monster now resembled nothing more than a giant dumpling.

"So...what was the point of all this?" Kirito asked. Leafa walked forward and patted the gray, furry hide.

"Hello, Tonky? What are we supposed to do now?"

There was no response. She smacked it a bit harder, then noticed a change in the texture of its skin. When they were riding on Tonky's back, the flesh had the resiliency of urethane cushioning, but now it was harder.

Alarmed, she put her ear to the furry hide, thinking it might have died after completing its purpose. Much to her relief, there was a steady, faint pulse echoing through the massive body.

So Tonky was still alive. In fact, the HP gauge in its yellow cursor showed that the wounds it had suffered at the hands of the three-faced giant were fully healed.

"Does this mean...it's just sleeping? While we're struggling to stay up all night?" She was about to yank on its fur in retribution for its cheekiness when Kirito called out to her.

"Hey, Leafa. Look up, it's really cool."

"Huh...?"

When she raised her face, the sight that greeted her was indeed stunning.

The conical shape of the World Tree's roots were now directly overhead. The black tendrils wove around a mammoth icicle that was roughly the same width as the vertical shaft below it. When she looked closer, there seemed to be some kind of structure within the icicle. She could make out tiny corridors and rooms carved into the ice, the flames within gleaming blue through the translucent surface.

"It really is incredible...If that's all one dungeon, it's got to be the largest in all of *ALO*," she said, unconsciously reaching toward it. There was at least two hundred yards of space between her and the bottom tip of the icicle, of course. Even an imp, with their underground flight abilities, couldn't reach that height.

"But how do we get up there?" she mumbled. Kirito seemed

about to say something, but before he could get the words out of his mouth, the pixie on his shoulder cried out.

"Papa, I'm getting a player signal approaching from the east! There's one…with twenty-three behind it!"

"…!!"

Leafa sucked in a large breath. Twenty-four players—clearly a raiding party hunting Deviant Gods.

This should have been the encounter they were waiting for. If they explained their plight, they might be allowed to join the party until they could safely reach an exit to the surface.

But the players heading toward them now had a very specific intention in mind.

Leafa bit her lip and looked to the east. After a few seconds, she heard the faint sounds of footsteps in snow. It was quiet enough that without her excellent sylph hearing, she wouldn't have noticed. She also didn't see anything—they must have been using concealment spells.

She raised her hand and began chanting a spell of revealing, but before she could finish, a spot, in open space about ten yards away, rippled like a liquid surface, and a single player appeared with a splash.

It was a man. His skin was so pale it was nearly blue, and his long hair was the same, marking him clearly as belonging to the undine race. He wore gray leather armor tooled with a fish-scale pattern, and had a small bow slung over his shoulder.

His scoutlike appearance told Leafa his role was reconnaissance, but the high quality of his equipment and his confident, supple grace told her this was a very high-ranking player.

The sharp-eyed scout cast her a steely glance, took a loud step in the snow, and then asked what Leafa was most afraid of hearing: "Are you going to hunt that Deviant God or not?" He was, of course, referring to Tonky, curled up next to them.

When she did not immediately respond, the man's eyes narrowed. "If you are, then get on with it. If you're not, step away. We don't want you caught in our crossfire."

Before he finished speaking, a number of crunching footsteps sounded behind his back. The rest of the party had caught up to them.

If they're a mixed-race party based in a neutral zone, there might still be hope, Leafa prayed.

Her hopes were immediately dashed when she saw that the twenty-odd players cresting the snowy ridge had the same pale skin and bluish hair. This Deviant God raiding party was made up entirely of undines from Crescent Bay, far to the east.

If they'd been renegades of different races, perhaps they would have overlooked the sylph-spriggan duo. But these were representatives, the best and brightest of the undine players. If anything, they could gain honor points for killing Kirito and Leafa, who were of a different race, while the two of them couldn't possibly match up against twenty. They were lucky to have even gotten the warning that they did.

But we have to stand up and do the impossible now. Tonky treated us like a friend—we can't leave it to die, Leafa told herself. She stood between the blue-haired scout and the monster, and issued a gravelly warning.

"I know this is against in-game manners, but I beg your indulgence. Leave this Deviant God to us."

The man and his cohorts behind him chuckled uneasily. "It would be one thing to hear someone say that in a lesser hunting ground, but this is Jotunheim. You must have been playing long enough to know that claiming an area or a monster is 'yours' doesn't fly around here."

He was absolutely correct. In any other case, Leafa's reaction to someone else claiming ownership of a region or monster would have been the exact same as his. If the monster was currently engaged in fighting someone, that person or party had priority, but Tonky was simply curled up into a ball. Leafa and Kirito had no intention to fight with it, so they had no right to prevent the undines from doing so.

She bit her lip and looked down to the ground, unsure of what to do, when a shadow stepped forward—Kirito.

Leafa held her breath. He wasn't going to attempt to bluff them the way he had with General Eugene and the salamanders—or even worse, *fight* them, was he? He couldn't draw his sword against such a huge party.

It was insanity. They were hunting in Jotunheim, which assured that the twenty-four undines before them were among the best of the best. They were far tougher than the salamander party that ambushed the pair outside of Lugru; the gleaming heavy armor and sparkling wizard staffs alone told her that much.

But she was not at all prepared for what Kirito *actually* did.

The black-clad spriggan made no move toward the greatsword on his back. Instead, he folded at the waist and bowed deeply.

"Please," he croaked, deadly serious. "Its cursor might be yellow, but this Deviant God is our companion…our friend. It brought us here, even when it was at death's door. Please let it rest here as it wishes."

He bowed even deeper toward the blue-haired scout, whose eyes were wide with surprise. That was quickly followed by the largest expression of exasperation yet. The fighters behind him were openly laughing now.

"Come…come now. You're human players, right? Not NPCs?"

Hands wide, the scout stifled his laughter and shook his head. He took the beautifully ornate bow off his shoulder, drew a silver arrow from his quiver, and nocked.

"Sorry, but we're not here to lollygag around. The party was nearly wiped out by one of the larger beasts a few minutes ago. It took a lot of work to revive all the Remain Lights and regroup. We need to bag something to make this trip worth it. We'll count to ten so you can take your distance. Once the count is up, we'll pretend you aren't here…Mages, lay down buffs."

He raised a hand, and the mages at the back of the party began chanting spells. With each burst of colored light, the warriors at the front were enveloped in status-enhancing magic, in preparation for the battle ahead.

"Ten...nine...eight," the archer's countdown rang out through the sound of the spell. With her hands clenched so tight she could hear the bones creaking, Leafa shuddered and called out to her partner.

"Let's go, Kirito."

"...All right," he murmured and turned on his heel, walking to the west along the bottomless shaft. Leafa took to his side. The scout's countdown continued behind them.

"Three...two...one. Commence attack," he chanted mechanically.

They heard the piercing sound of fierce attack spells and the metallic clanking of heavy armor bursting into motion. Explosion after explosion sounded right behind them, and the ground rumbled beneath their feet. Leafa's ponytail was sent waving by the blast of hot air that hit her back.

After about thirty steps, Leafa and Kirito finally turned around to look.

The warriors had just started thrusting their swords, axes, and spears into Tonky's unmoving body. There were bright flashes and heavy shock waves from the impacts. The God's defense was formidable, but their expensive equipment struck right through it and took chunks of its HP bar down.

After several seconds of attacking, the eight warriors pulled back to a distance. A second round of attack spells went off, accompanied by arrows from the archers in the group.

The powerful explosions covered Tonky's trunk, which was over twelve feet tall even in its shrunken state. Pillars of fire burst from its skin, charring the silky short hair. Its HP continued falling, already 10 percent down from the maximum.

Between the rumbling blasts, they could hear a whistling, whirling sound.

It was Tonky. The Deviant God was warbling miserably, even weaker than it had when the three-faced giant was going in for the kill. Leafa turned her face away, unable to watch any longer...but what she saw tore at her heart even more.

Kirito stood with his fists clenched, and, peeking out of his front pocket, Yui was gripping the seam with both hands, her delicate knuckles white with force.

Her sweet little face was crumpled with agony. Large, round tears streamed out of her big black eyes. The sight of the tiny pixie, shoulders trembling, desperately trying to stifle her sobs, brought a hot sensation to the corners of Leafa's eyes.

If only this squad of undines had been a merciless PK gang!

Then Leafa could have hated them for what they were doing. She could have promised the dying Tonky that they would avenge its death.

But the undines were only performing the right of any MMO player. Ever since the development of the first tabletop RPGs in the last century, one goal was front and center in every game: killing monsters to earn gold and experience. Decades later, in the immersive full-dive format, that standard had not changed. The rules and manners of playing in *ALfheim Online* said that Leafa could not force these undines to stop.

In which case, what did it say about the existence of "manners" if they couldn't stand up to protect something, monster or not, that had traveled with them and shared their sentiments, even if only for a time? What was the point of rules if they couldn't even say, *Don't kill him, he's our friend*?

Leafa believed that in this world, the soul was free. She believed that emotions that could not be expressed in the real world were fair game in Alfheim. But it was as though the stronger players got, the better equipment they gained, the more they weighed down their own set of wings. She felt certain that even these undines, when they were brand-new to the game and unfamiliar with its ways, saw the frolicking, nonaggressive monsters in the wilderness and didn't wish to kill such sweet creatures.

Angst sat heavy in her stomach, not unlike a bar of lead. The

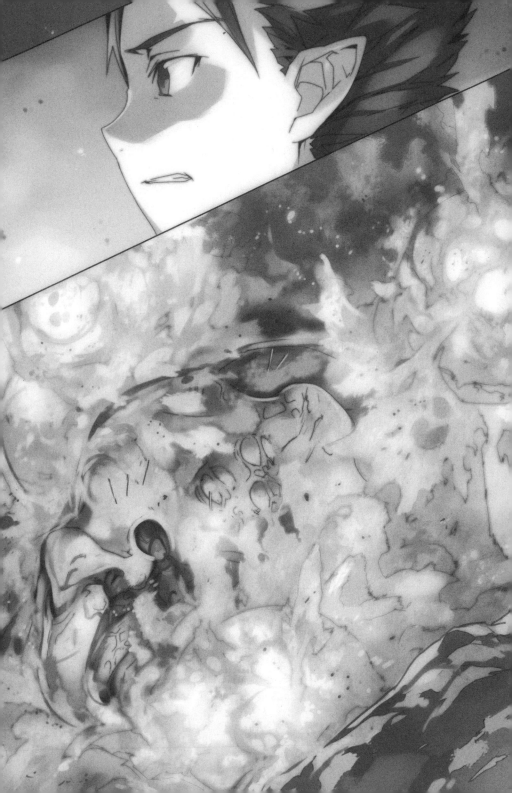

increasingly frantic sounds of attack were accompanied by ever-weaker cries from Tonky, who was wailing on and on. Its HP must be under halfway by now. It would take two minutes at the most—no, sixty seconds.

"...Kirito."

"Leafa."

They spoke together. She looked directly into the spriggan's black eyes. "I have to go save it."

"I'll go with you."

She was about to tell him to leave and head for Alne, but thought better of it. Once they charged into the fight, they'd be dead within ten seconds. There was nothing to be gained from it.

But standing there and watching the scene unfold went against Leafa's beliefs—and likely Kirito's, too. They'd saved Tonky from the three-faced giant, and Tonky had saved them in return. Perhaps the Deviant God was nothing more than a few lines of code tucked into a corner of the massive game server, following its simple instructions. But if she was going to stand and watch the murder of something she'd labeled a friend and given a name, there was no point to playing a VRMMO.

"Later today, I'll help you travel from Swilvane to Alne again," she said quickly. Kirito nodded, his hand on his sword hilt.

"Thanks...Stay out of sight, Yui."

"I will. Papa, Leafa, um...good luck." The pixie hid her teary face inside the pocket, and the two fighters drew their blades. One of the mages at the edge of the undine troop turned a suspicious eye at the sound.

They'd start with the low-defense mages, they told each other with a silent glance, and burst forward together. The snow at their feet shot high in the air, and the air around them shook with the force of their movement.

In a single breath, Leafa closed the distance and brought her long green katana down in a mighty, double-handed swing.

"*Seyyy!!*"

Her piercing cry was joined by the crisp swoop of her slashing sword. The green bolt of lightning that was her blade rocketed into the shoulder of the leftmost rear mage.

It was an unbelievably powerful blow, but the pale blue robe the undine was wearing was indeed an excellent piece of gear—the strike only took 30 percent of his HP. However, even as he tried to raise his staff to counter, a pitch-black light cut him straight across the chest. A split-second later, there was a heavy *wham!* as Kirito's greatsword took down another 40 percent of the mage's health.

The undine was tossed into the air without so much as a word, and Leafa's relentless combo finished the job. Gauntlet, gauntlet, helmet: The kendo strikes each took an additional 10 percent, reducing him to zero.

The mage's avatar vanished with a plume of blue water. Leafa brushed away the Remain Light and turned to the next foe.

Only now were the other mages, so consumed with their long-range attacks on Tonky, noticing that something was wrong. One of them screamed, his face aghast. "A-are you insane?!"

"You tell me!!" Leafa shot back, leaping through the snow.

Once the assault was obvious, the undine elites were predictably quick to react. They canceled the long-term heavy spellcasts and switched to short-range ones that were quicker to chant. But Leafa and Kirito's rampage was just a bit faster. They shielded themselves behind a second mage and alternated powerful strikes. The closer mages unleashed what spells they could, but they were all direct-fire missiles that Leafa and Kirito were able to dodge, getting nothing more than singed clothes.

Leafa dispatched a second foe with a heavy thrust, grimacing as she took one or two direct shots from homing spells. Kirito was already off and running toward his next target. He hoisted the sword that was almost his own height on his shoulder, held it for a second, then prepared to unleash an earth-splitting blast—

—when a silver arrow thudded into his left shoulder.

He turned with a start to see the leader of the scouts at medium range, already loading his next arrow with grim determination. The scout barked out a powerful order.

"Swordsmen, back! The mages are under attack!"

The second arrow roared through the air directly at Leafa's breast. The comet-tailed projectile was so fast, she could do nothing more than take the arrow to her left arm. With a heavy *thud*, she lost over 10 percent of her health. As she was tottering from the impact, a laser stream of high-pressure water magic pierced her right leg. It didn't hurt, but the unpleasant dullness caused her to grimace.

Kirito had just finished halving his third target's HP when he was swallowed up by an unavoidable whirlwind of ice. Leafa was racing over to cast a healing chant when she caught sight of a line of mages preparing a large-scale attack spell. Not only that, the heavy warriors who'd been surrounding Tonky were now bearing down on them at full speed.

So this is it.

Nearly fifty seconds had passed since they opened their assault. They'd put up an excellent fight against a group of this size, all things considered. Tonky would surely forgive them, knowing how hard they'd tried.

Crouched down and eyes closed, Leafa buried her face into Kirito's shoulder and waited for the final blow, whether by spell, arrow, or blade.

But before the sound of that blow, she heard a high, powerful whistle, like a recorder amplified a hundred thousand times. The chill air shook powerfully as the sound echoed off distant mountains and reverberated back. It could only be Tonky's voice, but this was nothing like the pitiful moans it was making moments ago.

So it's finally dead, Leafa thought, looking to the hill.

She saw its elliptical body gashed with countless deep furrows. They grew longer and longer, connecting before her eyes.

"Ah..."

She braced herself for the sight of that black blood spurting from the multitude of punctures. However, it was not blood that issued forth, but brilliant white light.

A resonant, high-pitched wail erupted with the circular explosion of light, enveloping the undine warriors, archers, and mages. Instantly, the auras of support magic and partially cast attack spells surrounding them evaporated into smoke.

A field dispel!

Only a small subset of very powerful monsters had that ability. It was much too strong for a wandering, low-level Deviant God. Unsure of what had just happened, Leafa, Kirito, and the twenty-two undines froze where they were.

As everyone watched, Tonky's trunk filled with a white radiance and then blew apart in a silent explosion. No, that wasn't quite right—it was only the hard, bulky shell that was disintegrated, because the growing mass of light was still attached, rising into a towering spiral.

The light spun higher and higher over their heads until it gently spiraled out and dispersed. The pattern resolved into what was clearly four sets of massive wings, glowing brightly.

"Tonky…" Leafa murmured in wonder. As though it had heard her, that same old elephantine face rose at the base of the wings. Tonky held its long nose high and flapped its wide ears.

With another high-pitched, whirling cry, the no-longer-jellyfish shape beat its eight wing lobes and rose into the air.

The round body was shifting, growing streamlined. The twenty appendages were still hanging from its belly, but now they were more like vines than the clawed legs from before. Leafa suddenly noticed that the tiny sliver of HP left was now blooming back toward full health.

Tonky's wings, held motionless about ten yards off the ground, suddenly turned a brilliant blue.

"Uh-oh," Kirito muttered. He covered Leafa's body and laid flat against the snow.

The next moment, terrifyingly thick bolts of lightning rained upon the ground from each of Tonky's tentacles. The undines were blasted by the tremendous lightning before they could so much as scream. The warriors at least seemed to weather the storm, but some of the archers and mages died in one hit.

"Retreat to the bottom of the hill! Group up for healing and rebuffs!" the scout leader ordered, taking quick stock of the situation. The survivors, now fewer than twenty, raced down the slope. The heavy soldiers formed a clanking wall of defense as the mages began casting behind them.

But Tonky's wings seemed to slide through the air after them, now glowing pure white.

The wailing sound erupted again, and another ring of light descended, nullifying all magic. Several spells in progress poofed into harmless dust.

"Damn!" the scout screamed in frustration, his facade of control slipping away. He tilted his bow upward and let an arrow loose. It left a trail of pitch-black smoke that settled heavily along the ground, cloaking his troop. "Retreat, retreat!!"

From Leafa's vantage point, she could see the undines peeling off to run pell-mell in the other direction. Once in full escape, their speed was impressive, and the blue fairies had soon vanished beyond the mounds of snow.

Now that Tonky had the power of flight, it could easily track the land-bound players if it so desired, but the Deviant God merely trumpeted in triumph. As the sound echoed away, it rippled all four wings on one side, facilitating a slow pivot in midair.

Tonky steadily flapped toward Leafa and Kirito until it stopped right over their heads. The elephant head was pale now, and the six eyeballs looked down on the humans.

"So...what do we do now?" Kirito asked. Leafa felt a moment of déjà vu.

It was the extended elephant trunk that answered his question, scooping them both up off the ground. Before she could even recognize that her suspicions were confirmed, Tonky tossed Leafa and Kirito onto its back. They landed hard on their bottoms.

Once they shared a look of recognition and put away their swords, Leafa rubbed the beast's white hide. It seemed to her that the hair was also longer and softer than it had been before.

"At any rate, I'm glad you're alive, Tonky," Kirito murmured.

Yui popped her head out of his breast pocket and clapped happily. "I'm really glad! Good things do happen if you stick around long enough!"

"Let's hope we stick around a little longer," he muttered, looking up and down from his vantage point.

Clearly, Tonky would take them somewhere from this point. But if the destination happened to be the bottom of this massive hole smack in the middle of Jotunheim, that certainly didn't make things any easier. Fortunately, after a brief whistle, Tonky instead headed for the impressive roots of the World Tree above.

With every rippling beat of its luxuriously furry wings, the massive Deviant God rose further up into the darkness of the cavern. It followed a gentle spiral trajectory until Leafa could see the entire vastness of Jotunheim below.

"Wow…"

She couldn't contain the marvel that passed her lips at the cruel, beautiful land of ice and snow.

Player flight was impossible in the cave, so Leafa and Kirito had to be the first to ever witness it from such a height. She was about to pull an image-saving item out of her inventory when she then thought better of it and clasped her hands instead. She could save a screenshot of the image, but nothing could preserve the feeling in her heart at this moment. It was a complex mixture of sadness and delight, frustration and liberation.

Whether it had any inkling of what ran through Leafa's heart or not, Tonky briefly dropped into a more leisurely spin before beating its wings mightily once more.

At first, Leafa's mind couldn't exactly process the sense of distance between herself and what she was seeing.

There was the icy-blue translucent cone that hung from the ceiling, as well as the net of black tubes that seemed to hold it into place—the roots of the tree.

Based on the distance blur, the gigantic icicle was at least two hundred yards tall. As they'd noticed from ground level, there were multiple floors visible within the structure, forming a dungeon of ice.

As she marveled silently at the incredible sight, Leafa suddenly noticed a golden light flashing at the very bottom of the icicle's sharp tip. She squinted, but still couldn't see it very well. Without thinking, she held up her right hand and chanted a quick spell.

A puddle of water vibrated in her palm, then crystallized into a flat piece of ice. Kirito peered over at her.

"What's that?"

"An Ice Scope spell. See that thing shining at the tip of the giant icicle?"

She squished her face cheek to cheek with Kirito's and held up the large lens. The golden light in the image wavered briefly before sharpening into focus.

"*Whoa!*" Leafa let out an extremely unladylike shriek when she recognized the source of that light.

Sealed into the tip of the icicle was a breathtakingly impressive longsword with a blade shining pure and gold. The sword's phosphorescent glow and fine decorations made it clear that this was a legendary weapon. Not only that—Leafa knew the name of this sword already.

"It's... the Holy Blade Excalibur. I saw a picture of it on the official ALO site... The only weapon greater than Eugene's Demon Blade Gram. It's the best sword in the game, and no one knew where to find it... until now."

"The best sword..." Upon Leafa's hoarse explanation, Kirito's mouth watered, and he gulped, comprehending.

Just above the sealed sword was a spiral staircase carved directly into the ice, and this path seemed to lead directly inside the dungeon within the icicle. If they conquered that dungeon, they could gain the server's ultimate weapon, a unique prize.

Tonky the Deviant God continued its spiral path around the side of the blue icicle, still rising steadily. Leafa finally tore her eyes away from the holy sword to see where they were heading, and noticed two things.

The first was a balcony extending out like a platform from around the middle of the icicle's considerable height. Tonky's trajectory would take them just by the edge, close enough that they could jump onto it if they wanted.

The other thing, far above it, was an individual root hanging from the ice-encrusted ceiling of Jotunheim, with a set of stairs clearly cut into it. The steps ran up to the ceiling and appeared to continue from there. It had to be an escape route up to the surface—to Alfheim.

The balcony on the side of the icicle dungeon and the staircase up to sunlight were not connected. If they jumped off now, they'd have a chance at the holy sword, but they'd likely lose their opportunity to escape the underground.

Kirito appeared to have reached the same conclusion. He looked back and forth between the balcony and the stairs. As the seconds ticked by, the balcony grew closer and closer. They only had twenty seconds left to decide...ten...

The two remained silent as Tonky slowly came level with the wide balcony. Leafa and Kirito flinched simultaneously, their VRMMO instincts screaming at them to jump.

But they did not, of course.

After sharing a look with Kirito, Leafa smiled apologetically and said, "We can come again later. With a bunch of friends next time."

"Agreed. I'm guessing this has to be the toughest dungeon in Jotunheim, anyway. We probably couldn't tackle it alone..."

"Oh, don't sound so crestfallen!" she laughed. Tonky continued past the balcony and began rising again. Below them they could see the shadow of a dreadful Deviant God emerging from the square entrance cut into the wall of the icicle. It was similar in shape to the humanoid three-faced giant that had attacked Tonky on the surface, only this one looked even worse.

Most likely, the other Deviant Gods within the depths of the most dangerous dungeon in Jotunheim were other humanoids. Which meant that Tonky and the other freakish Deviant Gods were at war with the humanoids, and were designed to escort human players. Perhaps that was why the three-faced giant had been trying to kill Tonky—to keep it from growing its wings.

If they'd joined a Deviant God hunting party arranged for that explicit purpose, they'd never have had the idea to save the jellyphant from its attacker. It was because she and Kirito had fallen down here alone that they'd experienced this in-game event... this friendship.

As Leafa pondered on these ideas, Tonky reached closer and closer to the ceiling. The dangling root with the steps carved into it was clearly in sight now.

With a wheezing whistle, Tonky spead its wings to slow down. The massive creature came to a gentle hover and extended its long nose to grab on tightly to the tip of the root, just next to the staircase.

Leafa got to her feet, the slightly swaying steps right in front of her. She grabbed Kirito's hand and stepped over to the bottom of the staircase.

As though recognizing the weight on his back vanishing, Tonky gently released its nose's grip and began to descend, rotating slowly. But its trunk's tip held in place for a while, and Leafa reached out one last time to grip it.

"We'll come again, Tonky. Take care, won't you? Don't let the other ones push you around," she whispered, then let go. Kirito touched the trunk next, and even Yui popped out of the safety of her pocket to squeeze a strand of Tonky's thick hair with her tiny hand.

"We should talk again sometime, Mr. Tonky," the pixie squeaked. The Deviant God ruffled a deep response and folded its wings. It dropped like a stone, growing smaller before their eyes.

With a final twinkle of feathers, the strange creature finally melted into the darkness of Jotunheim below. With its full-grown wings, it could fly to its heart's content, free from the harassment of others. One day, if Leafa stood at the lip of that massive hole in the ground and called its name, she felt sure that it would offer them another ride.

She wiped away the wetness in the corners of her eyes and gave Kirito a big smile. "C'mon, let's go! I bet we'll emerge in the middle of the Alne!" she chirped.

Kirito stretched his limbs. "All right, time for a final run, is it?...Though, hey, Leafa? Even after we return to the surface, let's keep the holy sword a secret between us."

"Oh, you just had to ruin this precious moment with that statement, didn't you?" She jabbed the spriggan on the shoulder and started vigorously jogging up the spiral staircase, still hand in hand with him.

The trip down had taken less than three minutes through the giant earthworm's digestive tract, but the hike back seemed much longer. Onward they climbed, their path lit by dimly glowing mushrooms. Leafa quickly gave up on counting the steps, and after ten long minutes, an actual beam of light was visible above.

They shared a look and started the final spurt. Jumping an extra step with each leap, Leafa popped out of the hole in the tree wall headfirst.

The sylph rocketed out onto a mossy stone terrace with such momentum that she flipped head over heels and landed butt first on the hard floor. After a brief squint, she hopped to her feet to take in the sight that lay before her.

It was the night view of a beautiful, stately, layered city.

Stone structures in the style of ancient ruins extended as far as the eye could see. The yellow bonfires, magical blue flames, and pinkish mineral lanterns twinkled and fluttered like stardust. Beneath the lights, a vast array of player silhouettes in every shape and size milled about: An equal ratio of all nine fairy races walked the streets.

After a long gaze at the glittering scene, Leafa looked upward. The shadows of branches and leaves were clearly visible against the deep blue of the night sky.

"...The World Tree..." she murmured, then turned to Kirito. "This is it. We're in Alne, the center of Alfheim. The biggest city in the world."

"Yeah...We finally made it," he nodded. Yui popped her head out of his pocket, her face shining.

"Wow...! I've never seen so many people in one place before!"

Leafa could say the same. It had never occurred to her that so

many players would have left their home territories to enjoy their own adventures.

The three sat for a time on the railing of the terrace, letting the bustle of the metropolis wash over them.

Eventually, they were awakened from their reverie by the heavy blast of a thick sound, something like a pipe organ. It was followed by a soft, feminine voice coming from the sky. The announcement was for the weekly round of maintenance that would shut off the server at four AM. Leafa had never heard this voice before—she'd never been online this late.

It's been one long series of firsts for me, the past two days. She swung her legs forward.

"I suppose that's it for today. Guess we should find an inn to log out," she said to Kirito, who nodded in agreement.

"How long does the maintenance last?" he asked.

"Until three in the afternoon."

"I see…"

He looked down briefly before tilting his head back to scan the sky. A vast distance above, the branches of the World Tree spread in all directions.

Kirito's black eyes narrowed and his mouth twitched. Leafa suddenly remembered his reason for being in Alfheim to begin with.

He was going to meet *someone* at the top of the World Tree. Who could it be? If it wasn't an NPC in a quest, then perhaps a staffer with the dev team, or…

But before she could come up with a better guess, Kirito was back to his usual expression. "C'mon, let's find an inn. I'm strapped for cash, so we can't pick a five-star hotel."

"That's what you get for showing off and giving Sakuya all your money. You should have kept enough for a room!" Leafa laughed, shaking off her previous curiosity. She looked down at Yui in her usual pocket perch. "You heard Papa. Is there a cheap inn around here?"

Oddly enough, the Navigation Pixie also seemed to be gazing

up at the branches with an expression of intent, but she soon answered with a smile.

"Yes, I think there's one just down that alley. A real slum!"

"Great, my favorite," Leafa groaned, her face twitching. Kirito marched right off without a care, so she had to rush to catch up.

There was a stirring in her chest despite the exhaustion of staying up so late. Leafa took one last look up at the World Tree.

But of course, she couldn't see anything among the branches sunken into the night sky.

6

In January 2025, Asuna Yuuki was held prisoner in more ways than one.

Her first cage hemmed her in with golden bars. It was a delicate and beautiful birdcage sized and outfitted for a human being, but nothing she did could break herself loose.

That was because the bars, though only a fraction of an inch thick, were not real metal, but virtual data made of ones and zeroes. If the system defined them as "unbreakable," even the largest hammer in the world couldn't put a scratch on their surface.

The second cage holding her prisoner was this entire virtual realm.

The world's name was *ALfheim Online*, abbreviated as *ALO*. It was a massive multiplayer online role-playing game—or in other words, a VRMMO—run by a company called RCT Progress.

ALO itself functioned as a completely normal online game, with thousands of ordinary customers who paid a monthly fee for access to the entertainment within. But behind that facade lurked a massive illegal and inhumane experiment hatched by one man's wicked hubris.

The basic engine that ran *ALO* was a replica of *Sword Art*

Online, the game that shocked Japan to its core from 2022 to 2024.

Ten thousand players of all ages were trapped within *SAO*, and a full 40 percent perished as a result. The game's developer, Argus, was completely obliterated by the damages caused, and maintenance of *SAO*'s servers during this time was left to the Full Dive Development Division of RCT, a massive electronics manufacturer. The man in charge of this project had not only spun off a copy of the *SAO* system for a subsidiary to develop and release to the public, he also succeeded in holding three hundred *SAO* players captive within the server, even after the game was beaten and everyone inside supposedly set free. These three hundred had their minds and souls held prisoner within the new *ALO* server.

This singular man intended to use those three hundred brains as test subjects for a new experiment: using the full-dive system to manipulate a person's memory and emotions.

At the same time, he'd trapped Asuna directly within the world of *ALO*. She was given an avatar body and placed far out of reach of any player: inside a birdcage that hung from the branches of the massive World Tree, which stood at the center of the world of Alfheim. He plotted to keep her there until he was officially wed to the comatose Asuna in the real world, and had secured his position as the heir to Shouzou Yuuki, CEO of RCT. Two months after the end of the *SAO* Incident, he was on the doorstep of achieving both those goals.

The man's name was Nobuyuki Sugou.

He was also known as Oberon, the fairy king who ruled over Alfheim.

━━∿∿∿━━

Asuna had gone to great lengths to secretly acquire the keycode number needed to leave her golden prison. Currently, she proceeded carefully forward, the sinking red orb of the sun to her left.

The walkway carved into the frightfully thick branch of the World Tree was etched with intricate patterns in its floor and half wall, which, combined with the handrails crafted of fresh shoots, played up the sheer fantasy of the setting. The occasional glimpse of decorative objects such as small birds and rodents animating themselves told her she was most definitely inside a game.

Thinking there was an unlikely but undeniable possibility of monsters, she walked cautiously. For several minutes she went along the path, until, brushing a curtain of the tree's leaves aside, she finally came to a gigantic wall that had to have been the trunk of the tree. A black hole gaped at the intersection of her branch and trunk like a giant knothole, and the path continued through it, into the tree. Asuna carefully approached the entrance, subconsciously slowing until her footfalls were silent.

Up close, she could see that while the outer aperture was irregularly shaped, just like a natural tree, farther in there stood a clearly artificial rectangular door. There was no doorknob, only a touch-pad plate. She traced a finger on the surface, praying that it wasn't locked.

The door slid open without a sound. She held her breath and peered inside to check that no one was there, then quickly darted inside.

It was a straight, off-white hallway that burrowed farther into the tree. The area was dim, with only the occasional orange light, spaced out mechanically along the walls. Unlike the beautiful, decorative exterior of the tree, this was a nearly blank environment, with only the barest effort involved in creating it.

It was as though the game world, without rhyme or reason, had suddenly turned into an office. The soles of her bare feet felt cold on the plain white floor. All of this told Asuna that she was finally reaching the enemy's stronghold. She bit her lip.

Nobuyuki Sugou was a man possessed by a different kind of madness than Akihiko Kayaba.

Despite being a powerful employee within a large company, he was using his influence to hold three hundred minds captive as subjects for a dangerous experiment. It was not the act of a sane human being. Desire and greed without end were what drove him. His instincts told him that he could never have enough. Asuna had known him since childhood—she understood this better than anyone.

At the moment, Sugou was filled with a certain amount of satisfaction, knowing that he owned a part of Asuna, and soon, her entire being. But he would fly into an uncontrollable rage when he learned that she had outwitted him and escaped her cage. He would make her suffer as much humiliation as he could manage and use her in his inhumane research. Just the thought made her knees go weak.

But if she turned back to the birdcage now, Asuna would truly be surrendering to Sugou. If it were Kirito, there would be no standing still here. Even without his swords...

She straightened her back and stared resolutely down the hallway, and then took one leaden step forward. Once she started moving, there would be no going back.

It seemed the hallway continued without end. There wasn't even a scratch on the walls, much less any joints between panels to break their monotony. After a time, she couldn't even be sure she was moving forward anymore. Only the occasional orange light overhead marked her progress, and with great relief she eventually noticed a second door far ahead.

It was exactly the same as the last one. She carefully touched the panel, and again the door slid open silently.

Behind the door was another identical hallway, only this one ran left and right. Disappointed, she stepped through, then was startled to see that when the door automatically closed, it melted perfectly into the wall without a trace that it was ever there. She felt around in a panic, but nothing made the door open again.

Asuna's shoulders slumped, but she told herself to forget the door—she wouldn't be going back, anyway. She raised her head and looked both ways.

This time the hallway was gently curved, rather than straight. After a moment of consideration, she took the right path.

Onward she walked, her quiet footsteps the only sound. Again her sense of movement began to melt away, until it seemed that she had simply been walking in loops around the same endless circle of hallway. And then, finally, Asuna spotted something that wasn't just another stretch of wall.

Stuck on the gray wall of the inside curve was a posterlike object. She raced over and saw that it was a map of the area. She consulted it eagerly.

At the top of the rectangular sign was a title in a plain font that read LABORATORY MAP, FLOOR C. Below it was a simple diagram. It showed that the structure had three floors, each of which was a big circle, and she was on the top floor.

There was nothing on Floor C except for the circular hallway. There wasn't even a marking for the straight tunnel that had brought her here from the birdcage. But on Floors B and A below, the inside of the circle was lined with various rooms and facilities: Data Viewing Room, Main Monitoring Room, Sleeping Quarters, and so on.

Access to the other floors was found at an elevator, located at the top of the circle on the map. The elevator shaft met all three circular floors, and continued down below that.

Asuna followed the straight shaft down on the map until it ended with a large, rectangular room. A chill ran down her back when she read the label: TEST SUBJECT STORAGE.

"Test subjects…"

The words left a sour aftertaste in her mouth.

This was clearly the laboratory for Sugou's illegal experiments. Hiding it all within a virtual game would certainly make it easy to conceal from the company. And if the secret was in danger of leaking out, the simple press of a button would remove all traces of it without a paper trail.

Knowing the purpose of his research, the term *test subjects* could only refer to one thing. They were the other former *SAO* players that Sugou still held captive. Through some means, he had their minds held within that storage room on the map.

After a long silence, Asuna turned and began to walk down the curving hallway again. She kept a quick pace for several more minutes until a plain sliding door came into view along the outside wall to her left. There was a plate affixed to the wall next it, upon which there was a downward-pointing triangle.

She took a deep breath and touched it with her finger. The door instantly slid open to reveal a small, rectangular room. She stepped inside and turned around, and came face-to-face with an elevator panel, just like any in real life.

After a moment's hesitation, Asuna pressed the lowest of the four buttons. The door closed, and to her surprise she felt a falling sensation. The small box carrying Asuna descended silently through the enormous tree, and after many seconds, the virtual sense of speed eased away. A crack that had not existed before opened in the middle of the smooth white door, and the two halves retreated into the walls.

As quietly as she could, Asuna snuck out of the doorway.

Before her eyes was another plain hallway no different from the ones above. She checked to make sure there was no one around, then started walking.

The outfit Oberon had given her was only a simple, sheer one-piece that offered little comfort, but she was glad to be barefooted now. If she were wearing shoes, she couldn't have avoided creating footsteps that would echo down the hall. Back in *SAO*, she would sometimes take the defensive hit and go barefoot, just to make it easier to ambush unsuspecting monsters from behind for extra damage.

Even outside of battle, back in the ruined sector of Algade, she'd play the "Sneak Attack" game with Kirito, Klein, and Liz, and with her light equipment and almost no sources of noise, Asuna always placed well. She'd never been able to land a back attack on

Kirito, so one time she tried going barefoot out of frustration. He sensed her wooden blade just before it hit him on the back of the head and easily slipped out of the way, then grabbed her leg and tickled her foot until she thought she'd die laughing.

It was that world she longed for now, even more than the real world that she couldn't be sure actually existed anymore. When she realized that tears were coming to her eyes, Asuna shook her head to get her feelings under control.

Kirito was waiting for her in the real world. The only place she truly belonged was in his arms. She had to keep moving to make that happen.

This hallway was not quite so long. She soon came across a tall, narrow door straight ahead. Asuna told herself that if this one was locked, she'd have to go back up into the laboratory to look for a system console. But contrary to her fears, the door slid open, just like the rest. She had to squint to block out the powerful light that came from within.

"…?!"

Once she could see inside the door, Asuna gasped.

It was a breathtakingly vast chamber.

She thought it resembled an enormous white event hall. It was hard to gauge the scale of the room, because the three walls in the distance held not a single detail to distinguish them visually. The entire ceiling was glowing white, and the similarly colored floor had neatly packed rows of short pillars, arranged together into a grid.

Once she was sure there was no movement inside, Asuna hesitantly stepped into the room.

From her position, there were eighteen rows of the pillar-like objects. If the room was a perfect square, that would make the total eighteen squared, or just over three hundred. She approached one of the pillars, the fear sharp in her throat.

The round pillar reached from the floor to Asuna's chest. It was just wide enough that she could fit both arms around it. Something was floating just off the smooth, flat surface of the top. It was, quite clearly...a human brain.

It was actual size, but the coloring was not realistic—it was made of some bluish-purple translucent material. The model was extremely fine, however. It looked more like a sapphire sculpture than a hologram.

Upon closer examination, Asuna saw that there were rhythmic pulses of light at various spots on the transparent brain, little lines that turned into colorful sparks at their end points. They were almost like bundles of extremely fine sparklers.

She watched, brows furrowed, as the spreading network of light suddenly pulsed stronger. The sparks went from yellow to red, flickering menacingly. A translucent graph below the brain was recording sharp peaks. The detailed log running next to the graph was full of numbers and symbols, along with the occasional word like *pain* and *terror*.

It's suffering, Asuna realized suddenly.

The brain right in front of her was agonized with pain, sadness, perhaps even fear. Those little sparks were screams. A faint image of the face belonging to that brain floated before Asuna's eyes like a vision, twisted to the extreme, the jaw open as wide as it could go, silently screaming over and over and over.

She fell backward, unable to stand the horrifying image. She flashed back to the Test Subject Storage label on the map and Oberon's phrase, *emotion-manipulation technology*. The two concepts overlapped and formed one terrible conclusion.

This brain and the hundreds around it were not computer-generated objects, but actual human minds—real-time monitors of the former *SAO* players. People who should have been freed at the end of the game, but who had somehow been spirited away to this place by Sugou's hand and subjected to inhumane research. This was a map of the manipulation of thoughts, emotions, and memories through their NerveGear.

"How...how could you do such a horrible thing..."

She covered her mouth with both hands. The research being done here was one of the great taboos, like human cloning. It wasn't just a simple crime. This was the destruction and desecration of the last vestige of human dignity: the soul.

Asuna craned her neck to the right. Six feet away was an identical pillar with another transparent brain floating on top. The construction was identical, but whoever this brain image belonged to, it was much calmer. The sparks were yellow with the barest tinge of red, and as slow as thick liquid.

On it continued, to the next row and beyond: a seemingly infinite array of prisoners, their crystal brains a spectrum of colors, each one screaming in despair.

Asuna fought down her impulse to panic and rubbed at the teardrops pooling in her eyes.

It was unforgivable. She'd make him pay. She and Kirito hadn't risked their lives to help Sugou undertake such a horrendous sin. She'd expose his crime and see that he was punished appropriately.

"Just hang on. I'm going to save you soon," she whispered, caressing the side of the anguished brain. She looked up again, eyes resolute, and strode with purpose through the rows of pillars farther into the room.

Just as she counted ten rows of pillars, Asuna heard something that sounded like a human voice. She instinctually dropped down behind the nearest source of cover and scanned the area carefully, trying to discern the source of the sound. It seemed to be coming from farther ahead and to the right. She snuck forward, almost crawling on hands and knees.

After several pillars, she noticed something odd ahead.

"…?!"

Asuna shrank back, blinked rapidly, then stuck her head out again.

The sixty-first floor of Aincrad was nicknamed "Bugland" by its players. As the name suggested, it was overflowing with insect-themed monsters, a particular type of hell to squeamish female players like Asuna. The worst were the giant, slimy bull slugs. Their black-spotted gray hides were covered with a slick substance, and each followed its target with three pairs of eyestalks of varied sizes, only to then attack with horrendous tentacles that extended from its mouth. In short, they were straight out of a nightmare.

Now, just a few dozen feet away from Asuna, two creatures that eerily resembled those bull slugs were having a conversation.

The giant slugs were watching one of the brains and excitedly discussing it. The slug on the right was screeching with delight, its eyestalks swiveling back and forth.

"Ooh! He's having another dream about Spica. The B13 and B14 fields are off the scale. Sixteen's pretty high, too… He's lovin' it."

The slug on the left, who was prodding the holo-window floating next to the test subject, replied, "Sure it's not a coincidence? Only his third time, right?"

"It's the emotional guidance circuit modeling, I tell you. I put that image of Spica into his memory centers, but this frequency is way over threshold, right?"

"Hmm. Guess we should raise the monitoring sample rate…"

Asuna shrank back into the shadow of the pillar, her skin crawling at the hideous slugs and their screeching voices. She wasn't sure why they had to take that appearance, but it seemed clear that they were Sugou's assistants in his inhumane research. Based on their conversation, they didn't seem to possess the slightest hint of a moral compass.

She clenched her right fist, wishing she had a sword in it. She'd show them the end they deserved.

Asuna retreated, trying to control the fires of rage that consumed her. Once she'd put some distance between herself and the slugs, she headed farther toward the back of the chamber. Carefully but quickly, she passed row after row of pillars until she was at the last line. There, she saw a simple black cube floating in front of the distant white wall.

It reminded her of the system console she'd once seen in the underground labyrinth below the base floor of Aincrad. If she could access that cube with administrator privileges, perhaps she could finally log out of this mad world.

There was nothing to hide her up ahead. Asuna took a deep breath to steel herself, then leaped forward out of the shadow of the pillar.

She raced over to the console as quickly and quietly as she could. It was only thirty feet or so, but it felt like a mile. She kept her feet running, trying desperately not to get tangled up, expecting to hear a shout from behind with every step—until, finally, she reached the console safely. Asuna spun around just in case—she could see the waving tentacles over the endless rows of pillars. The slugs were still lost in debate.

She returned to the console. The diagonally sloped top surface was black and quiet, but there was a thin slit on the right side with a silver keycard still stuck in the top of the slot. With a silent prayer, she grabbed the card and slid it downward.

A *ping* sounded and she ducked her head. A blue window and holo-keyboard appeared to the left of the card slit.

The window was filled with a variety of menus. She browsed the small English letters quickly, trying to hold back her panicked impatience.

She extended a trembling finger to touch a button marked TRANSPORT at the bottom left. Another window buzzed open with a full map of the laboratory area. This system would apparently let her jump to various rooms within the facility.

But she had no more business in this place. Asuna scanned the lists frantically until she caught sight of a small button that said EXIT VIRTUAL LAB.

This is it! she thought to herself and touched the button. Another window popped up. The small rectangle asked EXECUTE LOG-OFF SEQUENCE? with two buttons marked OK and CANCEL.

Please, God, she silently prayed, moving her hand to touch the button.

A gray tentacle wrapped around her wrist.

"...!!"

Asuna somehow held in the scream that threatened to burst out of her throat. She desperately tried to lower her finger to the button, but the tentacle was as firm as steel wire. When she tried to swing her left hand over instead, another tentacle caught it. Both of her arms were pulled up into the air until her feet left the ground.

Asuna's captor slowly turned her around in midair. As she feared, it was the giant slugs she'd passed moments earlier.

Four orange eyes the size of tennis balls swooped toward her on narrow stalks. The expressionless orbs gazed impassively at her, as though scanning her face and body. Eventually the left slug's round mouth slurped open to emit a screeching voice.

"Who are you? What are you doing? And how did you get here?"

Struggling to keep her fear under control, Asuna tried to answer as casually as she could. "Let me down! I'm Mr. Sugou's friend. He was letting me observe the area, and I'm just on my way out."

"Oh? Why didn't I know about this?" the slug on the right asked, two of its eyes tilting sideways in an apparent sign of curiosity. "Did you hear anything?"

"Nope. Besides, it'd be an awful idea to show this place to an outsider."

"Oh...hang on a sec..." A round eyeball stretched closer until it stared directly into Asuna's face. "I know who you are. You're the one Sugou's keeping at the top of the World Tree..."

"Oh, yeah. I remember that. Man, the boss has it made. Look at this cutie!"

"Ugh..."

Asuna looked over her shoulder and tried to hit the button with her foot, but a fresh tentacle from the slug's mouth reached out and caught her ankle. She wriggled, trying to break free, but it was too late—the prompt had apparently timed out, and the log-out window returned to the original menu.

"C'mon, don't make trouble now."

The slugs wrapped her in more and more tentacles until she

was truly immobilized. The thin, fleshy ropes dug into the soft skin of her stomach and thighs.

"Ouch! Stop...Let go of me, you monsters!"

"Well, that's mean. We're just in the middle of experimenting on deep sensory mapping."

"Yes. It took a lot of training to learn how to manipulate these bodies like this!"

Asuna's face screwed up at the unique dull pain of the virtual world, as though her nerves were coated with silk, but she managed to shoot back a response.

"Aren't you...supposed to be scientists?! How can you undertake such...such illegal, inhumane experiments and still live with yourselves?!"

"Personally, I think this is still more humane than exposing test animals' brains to open air and jamming electrodes into them. I mean, all they're doing here is dreaming."

"Yeah. Sometimes we even let 'em have a really wonderful dream. It's nice to spread the love once in a while."

"...You're insane..." Asuna choked. A chill running down her back. The emotionless slugs weren't a facade; it was their true form.

The slugs shared a look and began to discuss between themselves, unaffected by Asuna's retorts.

"The boss is on a business trip, right? You should go out and get some orders."

"Tsk, fine. Don't go having too much fun without me, Yana."

"I know, I know. Just get outta here."

One of the slugs released its hold on Asuna's body and used a tentacle to deftly flip through the console's menus. A few buttons later, the large creature silently and abruptly disappeared.

"...!!"

Asuna felt panic burning her body like a hot poker. She twisted and writhed with all of her strength. The exit to the real world— what she'd dreamed of for so long—was right next to her. The doorway was slightly open, and the light from the outside was shining through, beckoning her.

"Let go!! Let go!! Let me out of here!!" she screamed, but the slug's grip did not weaken.

"I can't do that; the boss would kill me. Listen, don't you get bored just being stuck in here with nothing to do? Have you ever tried fooling around on electrodrugs? I'm getting bored of just playing with dolls."

Asuna felt a cold, clammy tentacle brush her cheek.

"S-stop it!! What are you doing?!"

She tried to resist, but the slug sent more and more tentacles after her. They wrapped around her limbs and trunk and even began to slip into her dress.

Stifling her urge to shiver at the disgusting crawling sensation, Asuna let the strength drain out of her body, feigning the loss of will to fight. One of the eager tentacles approached her mouth. The instant it touched her lips—

Asuna raised her head and bit the ropy feeler as hard as her jaws could snap.

"*Gak!!* Yeowww!!" the slug screamed, but she only bit harder. "S-stop—ow! Okay, okay!!"

Only when she felt the tentacle under her clothes retreat did Asuna open her mouth. The injured probe slithered out pitifully.

"Damn, I forgot the pain absorber ran out..." it moaned to itself, eyestalks retreating. A white pillar sprang up next to it, and the other slug popped back into place.

"...What are you doing?"

"N-nothing. What did the boss say?"

"He was freakin' furious. Told us to put her back in the birdcage on top of the lab, change the door passcode, and keep her on twenty-four-hour watch."

"Damn. I was hoping we could have some fun with her first..."

Asuna's sight seemed to grow dark with despair. Her one-in-a-million chance was trickling through her fingers.

"Let's at least walk her back, rather than teleporting. I want to enjoy the sensation of her skin."

"You're such a weirdo."

The slug holding Asuna prisoner started turning slimily toward the entrance of the storage chamber. When both creatures looked away for a moment, Asuna quickly stretched out her right leg and deftly gripped the keycard stuck in the console's slot, pulling it free with her toes.

The window shut down with the removal of the key, but the slugs didn't seem to notice. Arching her back like a shrimp, Asuna managed to transfer the key from her toes to her hands, which were bound tight behind her back.

"C'mon, no struggling."

The slug hoisted her up and began slithering toward the exit.

The door of the birdcage slammed shut. The slug fiddled with the number pad and waved at Asuna.

"So long. Let's hang out if you manage to break loose a second time."

"I hope I never see you again," she said coldly, walking to the far side of the cage. They watched her regretfully, but eventually turned away and proceeded back along the branch.

Night had covered the land while she was inside the lab. As she watched the twinkling of the city lights far, far below, Asuna murmured under her breath.

"I won't let this stop me, Kirito. I won't give up. I'm going to break out of here."

She looked down at the silver card in her hand. It was probably useless without a console, but at the moment, it was her only hope.

Asuna strode over to the bed, and, pretending to stretch and lie down, she slipped the card beneath her large pillows.

She shut her eyes and felt the veil of sleep slowly envelop her exhausted mind.

7

Out in the yard dusted with snow, the embrace of the chill morning air was biting, but even that did not drive all of the fogginess from my head.

I shook my head a few times and headed resolutely for the wash station in the corner of the open space. I twisted the old-fashioned silver faucet and held out my hands to catch the falling water.

It was so cold, it seemed like the pipes should be frozen. But I splashed water on my face nonetheless, an attempt to force all of my nerves into activity. They screamed in protest, but were splashed a few more times before I tilted my head down and drank directly from the spigot.

As I was drying my face with the towel around my neck, the glass door to the house opened, and Suguha stepped out in her tracksuit. She was normally an excellent morning person, but today she looked as miserably half-asleep as I felt.

"Morning, Sugu," I said. She tottered over to mumble a greeting, blinking heavily.

"Morning, Big Brother."

"You look sleepy. When did you get to bed last night?"

"Umm...around four, I think."

I shook my head in disappointment. "C'mon, kids shouldn't be staying up all night. What were you doing?"

"Ummm...the Internet...and stuff..."

This took me by surprise. The old Suguha would never have stayed up until all hours on the Internet. She really must have changed in the two years I'd been gone.

"Just don't overdo it. Not that I have room to talk..."

The second half of that came out as a quiet mumble. Remembering something from last night, I said, "Hey Sugu, turn around."

"...?"

She did a half turn, her face confused and still half-asleep. I put my hand under the faucet to get it nice and wet, then grabbed the back collar of her suit and shoved a half-dozen freezing-cold drops down her unprotected back.

"*Pyaaaaa!!*"

Her screech echoed throughout the yard.

Suguha was still in a huff throughout all of our morning stretches and swinging practice, but her mood improved instantly when I promised to buy her a raspberry cream parfait drizzled with green tea and sweet-bean syrup from our local diner.

We'd both slept in a bit this morning, so once we'd finished our showers after training, the clock said it was already past nine. As usual, our mom was fast asleep, so Suguha and I cooked our own breakfast.

I was washing and cutting tomatoes into sixths, and Suguha was dicing lettuce, when she leaned over and asked, "What's your schedule for today, Big Brother?"

"Well, I've got something to do in the afternoon...so I'm thinking of visiting the hospital before then."

"I see..."

Once I'd learned of Asuna's plight, visiting her in the hospital every other day was my most important custom.

As a sixteen-year-old in real life, there was very little I could do for Asuna—basically nothing, actually. Holding her hand and praying was the best I could manage.

The screenshot Agil had sent me flashed through my mind. Thanks to that picture, I'd made my way into the virtual world of Alfheim and, after two days, was very close to the location of the girl in the photo, but I had no proof that it was Asuna. I could be searching for her in the wrong place entirely.

But there was *something* to that world—that much was certain.

Sugou wanted Asuna to stay under forever. His company was involved in running *ALfheim Online*. The character data for Kirito and Yui the mental-care AI, both from *SAO*, fit right into the server...I didn't know how all the pieces added up, but there was something there.

When the *ALO* server maintenance finished this afternoon, I would be challenging the World Tree in that land of fairies. Just the thought sent shudders of impatience down my back. It would be nearly unbearable to sit in my room, waiting for the maintenance to finish, wondering to myself if I was any closer to Asuna than when I started.

So before I did any of that, I wanted to touch the real Asuna, to feel her warmth. Sugou had warned me to stay away from her, citing her condition, but there was nothing he could do to stop me from visiting.

Once they were cut, we tossed the tomatoes, lettuce, and watercress in a bowl and stirred in some dressing. Suguha was quiet throughout, but she eventually gave me a serious look and asked, "Hey, Big Brother. Can I go to the hospital with you...?"

"Huh...?"

I paused, bewildered. Suguha had never actively tried to learn more about my experience in *SAO* before. I'd told her a bit about Asuna a while back, but nothing beyond that, not even my character's name.

I panicked slightly when I remembered that two nights ago, shocked by the story of Asuna's engagement, I'd broken down and cried in front of Suguha, but this time, I managed to keep my expression cool.

"Yeah...okay. I'm sure Asuna would like that."

Suguha nodded happily, but there seemed to be a shadow behind her smile. I gave her a close look, but she only turned around, carrying the bowl to the table.

Nothing odd happened after that, and I soon forgot about Suguha's awkward reaction.

"What's up with your school situation now?" she asked, crunching her veggies across from me at the table.

It was a reasonable question. At age fourteen, the fall of my second year of middle school, I'd been taken prisoner by *SAO* and had not escaped for two years, making me sixteen now. This April, I should have been starting my second year of high school, but I hadn't taken any entrance exams, and even if I wanted to, most of my memory was now stuffed with a vast amount of data related to *SAO*. It would take a long, long time just to forget all those item prices and monster attack patterns so that I could replace them with historical dates and English vocabulary words.

The fellow with glasses from the Ministry of Internal Affairs had actually mentioned something about this, but I'd been so concerned with Asuna that I didn't take in most of that information. I strained to recall the fragments that remained.

"Let's see...I think they said they were going to use an old school campus that was left empty after some recent consolidation to make a special temporary school for the students that came back from *SAO*. No entrance tests to worry about, and if you graduate, you'll qualify to take a college entrance exam."

"Ohh, I see. That sounds nice...right?" Suguha smiled for a moment, then scowled and mumbled, "I guess it does seem a little too convenient and unified, though..."

"Well spotted," I said, smiling. "I think that's exactly what the government wants. We were locked inside a game for two years with the threat of death. They're worried about the effect that might have had on our mental health. So I'm guessing it's easier for them to manage the situation by putting us all together like that."

"Aw, I dunno," Suguha mumbled, scrunching her face up.

I hastily added, "Well, regardless of any overmanagement, at least they're offering a safety net. If I tried to get into a regular old high school now, I'd have to spend the whole year studying all over again at a cram school. Of course, they're not going to force us to attend this temporary school, so I have the option of trying on my own, if I want…"

"I'm sure you could do it. You have very good grades."

"Had, past tense. I haven't done any schoolwork in two years."

"I know! I could be your tutor!"

"Oh? Maybe I should have you teach me math and information processing."

"Umm…"

I grinned at her look of awkward hesitation and popped the slice of buttered toast into my mouth.

In truth, I hadn't been in any state to think about school recently. With everything that had happened and Asuna's current plight, it was hard to think of myself as an ordinary student.

Even now, two months back into the real world, I sometimes felt lonely and vulnerable without my beloved swords at my back. There were no more monsters lurking, waiting to pounce, but I still felt that sense of anxiety. It would take a while to get rid of the sensation that I was actually Kirito the swordsman, while Kazuto Kirigaya—who attended school, took tests, and grew older—was only a persona.

Or perhaps it was because inside my head, I still hadn't seen the ending of SAO. I couldn't hang up my swords until I'd seen Asuna returned to this world. I had to get her back. Nothing could start until then.

I paid for two tickets at the terminal and we stepped off the bus, into the street. Normally I rode my bike to the hospital, but today I decided to give the workout a rest and take the bus instead.

Suguha blinked as she stared up at the hospital.

"Wow, it's so big!"

"You should see the interior. It's like a hotel."

I waved at the guard as we passed through the gate. The walk up the tree-lined hill to the hospital itself was surprisingly long, and it took several minutes for us to finally make our way into the dark brown building. Suguha, the very picture of good health, looked around curiously at the unfamiliar setting, so I had to drag her over to the desk for our visitor passes before making my way to the elevator. We got off on the top floor and walked down the empty hallway to the last room.

"This is it...?"

"Yeah," I nodded, sticking the passcard into the lock on the door. Suguha stared at the metal nameplate next to the door.

"Asuna...Yuuki...So her character name was her real name? Most people don't bother to use their own name."

"I'm surprised you know that. As far as I can tell, Asuna was the only one using her real name..."

I slid the card back out, and with a quiet beep, the orange LED turned green and the door opened. Instantly, the thick scent of flowers flooded out. I stifled the sound of my breath and walked into the chamber of the serene, sleeping princess. I could feel the tension in Suguha's body as she stayed right next to me.

I put a hand on the white curtain and said the same quick prayer I always did.

Then I slid it aside.

Suguha forgot to breathe when she saw the girl sleeping on the spacious bed.

For a moment, she thought it wasn't a person. It must be a fairy—one of the Alfs, the true fairies that lived on the top of the World Tree. Such was the otherworldly beauty of the sleeping girl before her.

Next to her, Kazuto watched in silence, until he finally took a short breath and whispered, "Let me introduce you. This is

Asuna...Asuna the Flash, vice-commander of the Knights of the Blood. Even at the very end, I could never match her speed and precision with a blade..."

He trailed off and looked down at the girl.

"Asuna, this is my sister, Suguha."

Suguha stepped forward and said timidly, "It's nice to meet you, Asuna."

The sleeping girl did not respond, of course.

She looked at the navy-blue headgear stuck to the girl's head. It was the same NerveGear that Suguha had looked at nearly every day, often with hatred. Only the three glittering lights on the front face of the apparatus gave any sign that Asuna was alive.

The deep, terrible pain that Suguha had nursed while Kazuto was locked in the game for those two years was something he was grappling with now, she realized. Suguha's heart quavered like a leaf floating on water.

It was too cruel that this inhumanly beautiful person's soul should still be locked away in some other, hidden world. She wanted to bring this girl back to Kazuto's side—to bring a true smile of joy to his face.

But at the same time, she couldn't stand to see the look on his face as he silently gazed down at Asuna on the bed. She was starting to regret having come here.

When she had asked to tag along today, Suguha had wanted to know what her true feelings were, once and for all. Ever since Midori told her the truth, an itch had developed within Suguha, underneath all of the regret and longing of the last two years. Was it the close love she felt for her brother, or the romantic love she felt for her actual cousin? What did she want from Kazuto?

I just want to be with him forever...as a close sibling.

But was that really all there was to it? Could she truthfully claim that she wanted nothing more than to train with him and eat at the table with him every day?

These were questions she had asked herself over and over since Kazuto's return two months ago.

She'd thought that by meeting the person who owned the innermost part of his heart, she might discover the answers. But as she stood in the golden, quiet hospital room, Suguha felt herself growing scared. She was afraid to learn those answers.

She was about to say that she'd just be waiting out in the hallway, trying not to look at Kazuto's face, when he suddenly took a step forward and she lost her opportunity to excuse herself. He circled around the bed and sat down in the chair on the other side. Now he was front and center in her field of vision.

He grabbed up Asuna's small hand, which was poking out of the white sheets, and stared silently at her sleeping face. When Suguha saw the look on his face, a sharp pain pierced her heart.

"..."

That look in his eyes. It was the look of a weary traveler in search of his fated lover after many long years...perhaps a journey that had begun in his previous life and that would continue into the next. Behind the gentle, caring light in his eyes, she sensed a deep, mad longing. Even the colors of his irises seemed different.

In that moment, Suguha realized what her heart truly desired, and that it was in a place she could never reach.

She couldn't even remember what she and Kazuto talked about on the way back home.

The next thing she knew, Suguha was lying on her bed, staring at the blue sky in the poster on her ceiling.

Her cell phone was beeping happily atop the headboard. It wasn't an incoming call, but an alarm she'd set last night before bed. The time was three o'clock, the end of the *ALO* server maintenance. The gate to the other world was open again.

She didn't want to shed any real tears. If she cried here, she knew she'd never be able to give up on this. Instead, she'd cry a bit in the fairy world. Leafa was always peppy and energetic; she'd be back to laughing in no time.

Suguha stopped the alarm and picked up the AmuSphere sitting next to it. She put it on, lay back down again, closed her eyes, and sent her soul soaring.

When the sylph girl awoke, she was in an inn room on the edge of Alne, central city of Alfheim.

Last night—actually, early this morning—Leafa had at long last escaped the underground realm of Jotunheim. When she'd climbed the stairs carved into the roots of the World Tree, she was right in Alne where she'd hoped to be. The knothole she'd climbed out of closed up behind her in seconds, and there would be no turning back.

After that, she'd checked in to the nearest inn, rubbed her fatigued eyes, and then rolled into bed. She fell asleep immediately, logging out of the game automatically. She didn't even have the strength to bother with reserving a second room.

Leafa sat up and went over to the edge of the bed. The bustle of town, the smell in the air, and even the color of her skin were different, but that stabbing pain deep in her heart had not vanished. She stayed hunched over, waiting for the pain to turn into liquid so it could drip from her eyes.

After a few dozen seconds, a smooth tone announced the appearance of another person next to her. Leafa slowly raised her head.

The boy in black's eyes went wide when he saw her, but he recovered quickly and asked, "What's wrong, Leafa?"

Something about that gentle smile, like a breeze in the night, reminded her of Kazuto. As soon as she saw it, tears sprang into her eyes and fell through the air like glittering beads of light. She tried to put a smile on her face.

"Well, Kirito...I...I've got a broken heart."

He stared at her with his midnight eyes. She was struck by the urge to tell this strangely old boy with the very young features everything—but she clenched her teeth and held it in.

"S-sorry, I shouldn't be telling you this personal stuff. I know it's against the rules to talk about real life here," Leafa hastily added, trying to keep the smile on her face, but the trail of tears did not stop.

Kirito reached out and put his gloved hand on top of Leafa's head, tenderly rubbing it back and forth a few times.

"You're allowed to cry when it's hard—there *or* here. There's no rule that says you can't express your emotions in a game."

There was always a bit of awkwardness around moving and speaking in the virtual world. But Kirito's soft, sympathetic voice and gentle hands were smooth as butter. They enveloped Leafa's senses and made her comfortable.

"Kirito..."

She gently laid her head against his chest. As each of the tears silently dripped onto his clothes, they evaporated with tiny glimmers of light.

I love my brother, she told herself, as if just confirming what she already suspected. *But I can't speak this feeling aloud. I have to keep it trapped deep in the deepest part of my heart. That way I might actually forget about it one day.*

Even if they really were cousins by birth, Kazuto and Suguha had been raised as brother and sister for years and years. If she revealed her feelings, Kazuto and her parents would be shocked and troubled. Not to mention that Kazuto's heart belonged to that lovely girl...

She had to forget everything.

Suguha, in the form of Leafa, let herself sink into the chest of this mysterious Kirito, and hoped that day would come soon.

They stayed that way for quite a while, Kirito rubbing Leafa's head without a word the entire time. Eventually, a bell began ringing in the distance, and Leafa straightened up, looking at Kirito. This time she was able to give him a proper smile. Her tears had stopped.

"...I'm fine now. Thanks, Kirito. You're very nice."

He scratched his head and smiled shyly. "I've heard just the opposite plenty of times. Gonna log off for today? I think I can manage on my own from here…"

"No, I've come this far. Might as well finish the job."

She leaped up off the bed, did a spin and a half to face him, and extended her hand. "C'mon, let's go!"

Kirito nodded and took it, that usual slight smile playing across the corner of his mouth. Then, as though remembering something, he looked up toward the ceiling. "Yui, are you there?"

Before the words had finished leaving his mouth, the familiar pixie appeared with a sparkling of light between them. She rubbed her eyes with a tiny hand, yawning majestically.

"*Fwaaaa…*Good morning, Papa, Leafa," she said, plopping down on his shoulder. Leafa took a good look at Yui and greeted her with a question.

"Morning, Yui. I've been wondering…do Nav Pixies sleep at night like everyone else?"

"Oh, of course not. But when Papa's gone, I shut off my input systems and organize and analyze my collected data, so I suppose you could consider that a form of sleep."

"But the way you were just yawning…"

"Isn't that a part of the human start-up sequence? Papa does it for an average of eight seconds every time he—"

"Enough of that nonsense." Kirito jabbed Yui's cheek with his finger, then opened his item window and placed the large sword over his back. "All right, let's go!"

"Okay!" Leafa agreed, slinging her blade across her waist.

As they left the inn side by side, the sun was just reaching its apex overhead. Most of the numerous NPC businesses were open, and the nighttime bars and mysterious item shops had Closed signs hanging from their doors.

It was just after three o'clock on a weekday, but because monsters and items were particularly well replenished after weekly maintenance, there were plenty of players active.

Leafa had been too tired this morning to notice, but with fresh eyes now she saw a score of surprises among the crowds.

The variety of races and players strolling around and chatting happily was stunning anew—she saw short, squat gnomes covered in metal armors and lugging huge battle-axes; tiny, harp-carrying pookas that barely reached her waist; and even mysterious Imps with purple skin under black-enameled leather. At one of the stone benches throughout the city, she found a red-haired salamander girl and a young, blue-haired undine man staring deeply into each other's eyes as a cait sith with a massive wolf meandered past.

The sight was much wilder and more chaotic than the uniform green theme of Swilvane, but that liveliness was full of a buoyant cheer. Even Leafa momentarily forget the throbbing in her heart and let a smile steal across her face.

She noticed that part of her was hoping the two of them would look like a natural couple here, then hurriedly squashed that feeling. Looking ahead down the street, she was greeted with a sight that beggared the imagination.

"Wow…"

Alne was a many-layered city, jutting up out of the ground in a conical shape. Leafa was only in the outermost ring, far from the center, but she was still able to see virtually all of the city in its many-ringed wonder.

Looming over the exterior of Alne, and made of something obviously different from the light gray rock of the city, were numerous incredibly thick, moss-green cylinders. Each one was nearly as wide around as a two-story building was tall.

These giant cylinders snaking all over the center of Alne were actually tree roots. Headed downward, they pierced all the way through the thick surface layer of earth to the underground world of Jotunheim. But as seen upward from Jotunheim, they wriggled into fatter and fatter lines until, at last, breaking free of the surface, they all met at a single point hanging above the center of Alne. In other words, the city of Alne aboveground and the giant ice crystal jutting from the ceiling of Jotunheim were in symmetrical locations, with similar designs.

Leafa looked farther up, her back shivering with electricity as she did.

The roots met to make up the base of a tree so large and thick that any attempts to capture its essence with mere words would fail. From that confluence, the trunk shot straight upward, its bark gleaming a golden green from colonization by moss and other flora. And yet, the entire tree seemed to grow more and more bluish as it stretched deeper into the sky. Even higher than the sky's blue, the branches were shrouded in a white haze—not mist, but clouds. Said clouds were a visual representation of the flight altitude limit, but the branches shot straight through them and far above.

Just before they turned invisible against the blue and white of the sky, the limbs could be faintly seen sprouting into a wide radial pattern. Each branch grew thinner and thinner until lace seemed to cover the sky, all the way over to the outer edge of the city where Leafa now stood. Based on the width of the lower limbs, the canopy of the tree had to extend through the atmosphere and into space—if such a thing even existed here.

"So that's...the World Tree," Kirito said beside her, his voice faint with awe.

"Yeah...It's amazing..."

"And there's another city on top of the tree? Which is where..."

"We'll find the fairy king Oberon and the alfs, spirits of light. Supposedly, the first race to have an audience with him can be reborn as them."

"..."

Kirito stared silently up at the tree, then turned to her with a hard look on his face.

"Can you climb the exterior of the tree?"

"The area around the tree is off-limits, so apparently not. Plus, if you tried to fly, your wing power would run out long before you got up there."

"I thought you mentioned some people who stood on each other's shoulders in an attempt to reach the branches..."

"Oh, that," Leafa chuckled. "Apparently they got pretty close, but the GMs panicked and put in a fix to prevent it from working. Now there's a hard-coded barrier just above the cloudline."

"Oh...Well, let's go see the roots."

"Roger!"

They nodded in agreement and headed down the main thoroughfare.

After several minutes of weaving through the mixed parties on the road, a large stone staircase leading up to a gate came into view. Through it lay the center of Alne, which made it, in turn, the very center of the world itself. From here, the view of the World Tree towering above was nothing but a giant wall.

They were climbing the steps with awe, about to walk through the gate, when suddenly Yui's face appeared from the top of Kirito's pocket. She was gazing upward with an unusually intense expression.

"H-hey...what's the matter?" Kirito muttered, trying not to tip off anyone around them. Leafa watched the little pixie curiously. But Yui simply stared silently toward the top of the tree, her eyes wide. After several seconds, her tiny lips parted and croaked.

"It's Mama...Mama's there."

"Wha...?" Now it was Kirito's turn to stare. "Really?!"

"I'm sure of it! That's Mama's player ID...Her coordinates are directly overhead!"

Kirito turned a burning stare up to the sky. His face was pale, and his teeth were clenched so hard, Leafa could practically hear them grinding.

Suddenly, his wings spread. The clear gray surface flashed white for an instant, and with an explosive *bang!* he disappeared from the spot he was standing.

"Hey—wait, Kirito!" Leafa called out hastily, but the boy in black was rocketing upward and accelerating. Leafa hurriedly spread her wings and took flight after him, completely bewildered.

Vertical zooming and diving were Leafa's forte, but even she couldn't catch up to Kirito, who seemed to be equipped with rocket boosters. The black shape grew smaller and smaller before her eyes.

It took only seconds to thread through the countless spires that towered over the center of Alne and into the sky above the city. Players lounging on the high terraces followed the sight with curiosity, but Kirito merely darted past their noses on his way ever higher.

Eventually there were no more buildings in sight, only the greenish-gold cliff that was the trunk of the tree. Kirito raced parallel to the surface like a black bullet. The white clouds enshrouding the trunk were growing closer and closer. Leafa chased desperately, bracing herself against the wind pressure on her face.

"Be careful, Kirito! The wall's coming up!"

But Kirito didn't seem to hear. He was like an arrow attempting to split the sky, flying with enough force to tear a hole in the fabric of this virtual world.

What drove him to do this? Was the person atop the World Tree really this important to him? Yui had mentioned a "Mama." Was it a woman, then? Was the person Kirito sought so desperately actually his—?

Suddenly, Leafa's chest twinged. It was a similar but distinct pain to the one Kazuto made her feel.

She lost her concentration, and her ascending speed dipped. Leafa shook her head to clear her thoughts, and put all of her mind into her wings.

A few seconds behind Kirito, she reached the thick cloud layer. Her vision went white. If the story she'd heard was correct, the unbreachable altitude was set just above the clouds. She raced through them, slowing only a little.

Suddenly, the world went blue. There was endless sky above in a perfect cobalt-blue shade that just wasn't visible from the ground. Overhead, the World Tree stretched its branches as though supporting the heavens. Kirito was going even faster than before, heading straight for a branch.

An explosion of rainbow color erupted around him.

Just a few moments later, a shock wave ripped through the air like a peal of thunder. Kirito had slammed into the invisible wall and now plunged lifelessly through the air like a black swan hit by a hunter's shot.

"Kirito!" she screamed, rushing in his direction. If he fell all the way from this height, not only would he lose all his HP, the ill effects would plague him in the real world for quite a while after logging out.

But before she reached him, Kirito seemed to have snapped out of it. He shook his head a few times and began rising again. Another collision with the barrier, and another impotent burst of light.

Finally at his level, Leafa grabbed Kirito's arm and shouted, "Stop, Kirito! It's impossible! You can't get any higher than this!"

But his eyes were filled with a mad light, and he attempted to charge yet again.

"I have to do it...I have to go!!"

A thick branch of the World Tree split the sky in the direction he was looking. It was certainly in much clearer view than it would be from the surface, but the system's level of detail made it clear the object was still quite far away.

Yui darted out of Kirito's pocket. She sped upward on her own, leaving a trail of sparkling light behind.

Of course! A Nav Pixie's part of the system, Leafa thought momentarily, but the invisible barrier repelled even her tiny body. The spectrum of light rippled outward like the surface of water, pushing Yui away.

But with a sense of desperation that seemed totally unlike a programmed object, Yui pushed against the surface and shouted, "I might be able to reach her with a warning mode alert...Mama! It's me! Mama!!"

"...!!"

A faint shout reached Asuna's ears, and she lifted her head from the table.

She looked around frantically, but there was no one else in the golden cage. The sky-blue birds that came to frolic at times were nowhere to be seen. There was only sunlight shining through the bars of the cage, casting shadows.

She put her hands back on the table, certain it was a figment of her imagination.

"...Mama...!"

That time it was clear. Asuna leaped to her feet, kicking the chair backward.

It was the voice of a young girl, as delicate as the plucking of a fine harp. The sound struck Asuna's distant memories and reverberated throughout her mind.

"Y...Yui, is that you?" she whispered, then raced to the wall of the cage, clutching the golden bars and frantically searching the vicinity.

"Mama...I'm right here...!"

The voice seemed to echo directly inside of Asuna's head, so she couldn't tell which direction it was coming from. But, instinctively, she could sense that it was coming from below. No matter how hard she stared, she could see nothing through the white cloud layer surrounding the tree below, but that was the source of the voice.

"I...I'm up here!" Asuna shouted with all of her lungs. "I'm up here, Yui!!"

If Yui, her "daughter" from *SAO*, was here, then *he* must be, too...

"...Kirito!!"

She had no idea if she was loud enough to reach them. Asuna looked around the cage, desperate to find something aside from her voice that would signal her presence.

But she already knew that every object in the birdcage was positionally locked into place and couldn't be thrown out of the cage. Long ago she'd attempted to send a message to the players below about her presence using teacups or cushions, but it hadn't worked. She clutched the bars in frustration and desperation.

No...

There was one thing—one object that hadn't existed here before. An irregularity in the otherwise pristine prison.

Asuna ran back to the bed and reached under the pillows, pulling out the small silver keycard. She returned to the edge of the cage and hesitantly reached out, clutching it in her hand. Previously, she'd been rebuffed by an invisible wall that refused to let anything through.

"...!!"

Miraculously, her right hand felt no resistance as it passed out of the cage. The clear silver card glittered as it caught the sunlight.

Kirito... please notice me!!

She opened her hand without hesitation. The card dropped through the air silently, glinting as it fell straight toward the clouds.

I slammed my fist against the invisible wall, writhing in frustration. My hand shot back as though rebuffed by a powerful magnetic field, and a rainbow ripple extended through the air from that spot.

"Damn... What the hell is this!" I rasped through gritted teeth.

I'd come so far—I was so close. The cage that held Asuna's soul prisoner was just beyond my reach. And now my way was blocked by the unfeeling, unassailable wall that was the system's *programming.*

A terrible, destructive urge pierced straight through my entire being, and then burst forth like white-hot fireworks. Two days of logging in to *ALfheim Online*, religiously following its rules in my quest to reach Asuna…It was as though all the frustration and panic I'd built up exploded at once. I bared my teeth and reached over my back, intent on the handle of my sword.

That was when it happened.

Through the rage burning up my vision, I saw a small light, flickering above.

"…What's that…?"

I stared at the light, anger momentarily forgotten. The glittering object was slowly, slowly falling toward me. It was like a lone snowflake fluttering in midsummer sky, or a wafting feather of dandelion fuzz settling down after a long journey.

Still hovering in midair, I let go of the sword hilt and reached out toward the light with both hands. After several endless seconds, the silver object fluttered down into my grasp. I clutched it to my chest and carefully opened my grip, sensing a somehow familiar warmth.

Yui looked over from the left, Leafa from the right. Like them, I could only gaze silently at what I held.

"…A card…?" Leafa murmured. It did indeed appear to be a flat, rectangular card. The translucent silver surface bore no words or markings to identify it. I glanced at Leafa.

"Do you know what this is, Leafa?"

"No…I've never seen anything like it in the game. Try clicking it."

I followed her suggestion, tapping the surface of the card with my fingertip. But unlike any other object that appeared within the game, there was no popup menu.

Yui leaned forward to get a closer look and gripped the edge of the card.

"This looks like…a system administrator's access card!"

"…?!"

I held my breath, squinting at the card. "So…I can exercise GM privileges with this?"

"No...In order to access the system from within the game, you'll need the console this corresponds to. Even I can't call up the system menu on my own..."

"I see. But there's no way something like this would fall down without a reason. I have a feeling..."

"Yes. Mama must have sensed us and dropped it down to us."

"..."

I clutched the card. Just moments earlier, Asuna had been holding it. It was almost as though I could feel her will within it.

Asuna's fighting, too. She's doing her best to resist, to escape this world. There must be more that I can do.

I fixed Leafa with a stare. "Where's the gate that's supposed to lead to the interior of the World Tree? Show me."

"Um...that's in the dome beneath the roots of the tree," she said, looking concerned. "B-but you can't go. It's protected by guardians, and even full-size raid parties haven't been able to get past them."

"I still have to go."

I slipped the card into my chest pocket and took Leafa's hand.

The sylph girl had saved my behind on many occasions. I came to this world full of panic, not knowing left from right, and I'd never have come so far, so fast, without her knowledge and her energetic smile. I knew that someday, I ought to tell her the truth in real life and thank her properly. It was with this thought in mind that I said what came next.

"Thank you for everything, Leafa. I'll tackle what comes next alone."

"...Kirito..."

She looked ready to cry. I squeezed her hand and let go, backing away with Yui on my shoulder.

With one last look at Leafa, her long ponytail swaying in the air, I bowed deeply and turned around.

By folding my wings, I put acceleration into my drop and headed for the very bottom of the World Tree. After a few dozen seconds of almost-blinding descent, the complex shape of Alne came into view at the foot of the tree. Spotting a particularly large terrace between two roots in the city's top section, I prepared to land.

I spread my wings wide to catch the air and slow my descent as I gauged where to land. Despite my best efforts to cushion the impact, my outstretched feet hit the stone hard enough to cause a small blast. The other players lounging on the terrace turned to look at me with startled faces.

When they had all turned back to what they'd been doing before, I inclined my head toward my shoulder. "Yui, can you tell how to get to this dome?"

"Yes, it should be just up the stairs ahead. Are you sure you want to do this, Papa? Based on all the information, it should be nearly impossible to break through the gate."

"I've got no choice but to try. Besides, it's not like failing will be fatal."

"That's true, but…"

I rubbed her lightly on the head. "Besides, if I have to waste another second not trying, I'm going to go crazy. Don't you want to see Mama?"

"…Yes," she responded meekly. I poked her cheek and started heading for the large staircase ahead.

The area at the top of the wide stone steps seemed to be the very top level of Alne. The roots of the World Tree, which snaked up and over the massive conical bulk of Alne, all converged directly ahead, into one titanic trunk. But the diameter of it was so vast that from here, it merely looked like a curved wall.

But a stretch of that wall was decorated with two massive statues of fairy knights, ten times taller than any player. Between them was a stone door adorned with fine carvings. For being the starting point of the game's final story quest, it was remarkably absent of any players. By this point, the supposed impossibility of the quest must have been common knowledge throughout the population.

But I had to get past this door and its guardians to the gate.

Hang on, Asuna. I'll be there soon, I told myself, etching the words into my heart.

A few hundred feet later, I was standing in front of the massive door when the stone statue on the right began to rumble with movement. I quickly turned around, taken aback, and saw that the eyes beneath the helmet were glowing palely. The statue opened its mouth and a voice like rolling boulders emerged.

"O warrior ignorant of the celestial heights, dost thou seek entry to the castle of the king?"

At the same time, a yes/no prompt appeared, asking if I wished to initiate the final quest. I pressed YES without hesitation.

This time, it was the statue on the left that boomed, "Then prove thy wings can encompass the very sky above."

As the distant thunderfall of its voice died away, the large door split down the center. Its two halves slowly rumbled open. The ominous sound made me think of the terrible memories of fighting floor bosses in Aincrad. The unbearable tension of those battles came back to me, stealing my breath and sending a chill down my back.

I had to tell myself that dying here was not permanent. Now that Asuna's freedom hung on the outcome of this battle, it was truly the most important task I'd yet tackled.

"Here we go, Yui. Be sure to keep your head low."

"Good luck, Papa," she squeaked from my pocket. I gave her one last rub and drew my sword.

The rumbling finally stopped when the thick stone door was open all the way. Only darkness lay beyond it. I took a step inside, wondering if I should use my night-vision spell, but before I could raise my hand, a brilliant beam of light shone down from above, causing me to squint.

It was an unbelievably enormous round dome. The shape reminded me of the boss chamber on the seventy-fifth floor of Aincrad, where I'd fought Heathcliff, but this was several times larger across than even that.

I was apparently inside the tree now, as the floor seemed to be made of a lattice of tightly woven roots. At the outer edge of the space, the vines grew over the walls and stretched upward to form the ceiling. They grew more sparse the farther overhead they went, forming stained-glass patterns that allowed in light from above.

And at the very apex of that dome was a circular door. The ring-shaped gate was carved with delicate reliefs and composed of four wedge-shaped wings of stone that met at its center to make a cross. The route up into the tree was clearly through there.

I hefted my sword with both hands. Took a deep breath. Tensed my legs. Spread my wings.

"Go!!" I shouted to brace myself, and leaped with all my strength.

Not even a second into my flight, the luminescent spots in the ceiling began to morph. One of the shining windows bubbled forth as though giving birth: before my eyes, the light seemed to drip downward into the form of a human being, complete with arms, legs, four wings, and a roar in its lungs.

It was a gargantuan knight clad in silver armor. Its face was hidden behind a mask like a mirror. And in its hand was a sword even larger than mine. This was clearly one of the guardians Leafa had warned me about.

The guardian knight's mirror face turned to look at me as I raced upward, and with another gutteral roar, it dove.

"Outta my waaaay!!" I screamed in response and swung. As the distance between us closed to nothing, I felt the cold sparks in my head return—that familiar feeling of all my senses accelerating that I'd tasted so many times in *SAO*'s death matches. At the reflection of myself in the guardian's mask, I swung the broadsword with all my strength.

When our blades collided, a brilliant light ripped through the open space like lightning. My foe attempted to recover his balance and brandish the sword for another overhead slash, but I followed my blade's momentum and plunged it into his chest.

I grabbed the neck of the massive knight twice my height and pulled in close.

When fighting CPU-controlled monsters, the common strategy was to keep an eye on the damage-causing reach of the enemy's weapon and maintain a distance at least that wide, but against such a large enemy, even a so-called safe distance would leave me with blind spots. Staying in my current location was dangerous, but I could at least buy enough time to regain my footing.

I pulled back the sword with my right hand and put the tip against the guardian knight's throat.

"*Raaah!!*"

Thrusting my wings at full force, I shoved the sword with all of my might. There was the heavy *chunk!* of a hard object being split, and the blade thrust deep into the knight's neck.

"*Grgaaah!!*"

For the guardian's divine appearance, the scream that erupted from its throat was positively bestial. Its entire body froze, wreathed in pure white End Flames, and shattered.

I can do this! I screamed to myself. Statistically, this guardian was far from a proper floor boss in *SAO*. In a one-on-one fight, I had the advantage.

I brushed the white flames away and looked up to the gate— then felt my face grimace. Nearly every one of the countless stained-glass windows scattered throughout the still-distant dome was producing its own white knight. There were dozens of them—hundreds.

"*Aaaaah!!*" I bellowed, more to whip my frightened wits back into shape than anything. I would cut them all down, no matter how many there were. I beat my wings and raced upward.

Several of the new guardians descended to block my path. I set my sights on the closest one and swung again.

This time I focused on the point of the enemy's sword as it slashed diagonally down at me. I stretched to evade its path, trying to avoid a collision of our blades, which would knock

me motionless for precious moments. The maneuver wasn't perfect, and I felt the sensation of damage suffered as it clipped my shoulder, but I ignored it and trained my every nerve on counterattacking.

My giant blade struck the guardian's silver mask directly, splitting it in two. But the next foe was already descending through the white flames that erupted from its disintegrating body.

I gritted my teeth when I saw that this one's sword was already in an attack trajectory. Judging that I didn't have the time to evade, I held up the back of my left fist to deflect the swing. The resulting shock seemed to reverberate to the bone, and I saw my HP bar lose a full tenth of its value. But the deflection was successful at keeping the enemy's blow from my body, and the momentum left the knight unbalanced. I brought my sword down on its neck.

Because my attack speed had been sapped by the force of the enemy's blow, this swing was not a one-hit kill. Meanwhile, a new guardian swooped in from the right. I twisted around to meet the fresh threat and used the spin to kick the wounded knight's mask with a booted heel.

Thankfully, my avatar had inherited the Martial Arts skill data of *SAO* Kirito—a skill that was nearly useless in *ALO*—and the resulting blow was strong enough to finish the job. The guardian burst into flame, the death effect distorting its bellow of pain.

In just the nick of time, I was able to stop the third knight's swing with my sword.

"*Seyaaa!!*"

I walloped the knight's mirror mask with my left fist. It splintered with a sharp *crack*, and the creature roared in agony.

"Fall! Fall!!" I screamed. I was possessed with a burning desire for destruction that hadn't been present during the pitched battle against the undine warriors in Jotunheim early this morning. I thrust my sword against the knight's neck and punched with my left hand, over and over.

This was the world I'd once lived in. Wandering alone in the depths of a dungeon, my soul battered by a constant stream of deadly battles, swinging my sword as though to build my own gravestone out of the corpses of monsters.

My fist finally broke through the mask, and a shining, sticky liquid sprayed outward. I followed the voice inside me that demanded murder, plunging my hand farther into the light. When my entire arm burst through the back of the guardian's head, its body crumbled away into the familiar white flames.

My heart had been as hard and dry as stone back then. Beating the game and freeing all of the players was the furthest thing from my mind. I shut out all other souls, seeking only the next battleground.

Another four or five knights swooped down on me, brandishing shining blades and screeching like monstrous birds. A fierce grin stretched across my lips as I snapped my wings and plunged into their midst. My nerves trembled at the feel of the ferocious acceleration, and electric-blue sparks danced across my vision— the pulse connecting my brain to my false body.

"*Raaaahhhhh!!*"

With a war cry, I swung the massive sword in a straight, two-handed swipe. Their weapons deflected backward, and I cartwheeled through the air, using the acceleration to strike at their necks. Two dull *thuds* later, a pair of mirrored heads flew free. The flames of their deaths were like white thorns raking my nerves, and they only built up the blaze within me.

It was only in the arena of death that I could know I was alive. Only by throwing myself into hopeless battles, pushing myself to the absolute limit until I finally collapsed, could I live up to what I owed those who had died before my eyes.

I redirected myself without stopping the rotation's momentum, striking at the chest of another guardian, my right foot like a drill. The resulting *crunch* had an unpleasant, damp softness to it, but I shot straight through the guardian's body as it burst into flames. Two blades came from left and right as I finally came to a stop. I used my sword to block the right and my other forearm to block the left, ignoring the HP cost.

Wasting no time, I grabbed the right guardian's wrist.

"Grrruaahh!!" Howling, I swung the creature high overhead and into the one on the left. A heavy thrust through both bodies, and they were dead.

No matter how many of them came for me, I would keep fighting. Just as I had been once before, I would be cleansed by the flames of slaughter, my heart growing harder and sharper...

No—that's not it...

There were people out there who had done their best to give water to my parched soul. Klein, Agil, Silica, Lisbeth...and Asuna.

I...I'm here to save Asuna, and finally bring an end to that awful world...

I raised my head and looked at the dome. The stone gate was surprisingly close. But when I tried to fly higher toward it, something whirred over and pierced my right leg.

It was an arrow of light, gleaming coldly. A rain of them poured down, as though waiting for the moment I held still enough to target. Two, three, they continued to land, rapidly draining my remaining HP.

I scanned the area quickly and saw that some of the guardians had fanned out at long range, left hands raised, chanting spells in those unpleasant, distorted voices. Another wave of glowing arrows whistled down upon me.

"Gaaahh!"

I swung my greatsword to deflect the arrows, but several more struck true, sending my HP into the yellow zone. I spared another hard look at the gate.

It would be very difficult to defeat all of those long-range attackers alone, so I charged straight for the gate, hoping to power my way through. The hail of shining arrows pierced my body, but the goal was just ahead. I gritted my teeth against the blows and stretched out my left hand for the stone door...

But just seconds away, my back was jolted by a powerful shock. I turned back to see a guardian at point-blank range, mirror mask twisted in a triumphant grin, its massive sword stuck into my back. I lost my balance and all slowed down.

Like white vultures, a dozen knights swooped in for the kill from every direction. A hail of dull *thuds* rocked my body as their swords struck true over and over. I didn't even have time to check my HP.

A vortex of black fire, tinged with blue, swirled around me. It took me a few moments to realize that I was seeing my End Flames. Small purple words floated up against the backdrop of fire: *You are dead.*

In the next instant, my corpse shot apart.

Like switches being flipped off, I quickly lost all physical sensation. I had a moment of uncontrollable panic as my memory flashed back to the final battle on the seventy-fifth floor of Aincrad, and the moment Heathcliff and I killed each other.

But, of course, this time I did not lose consciousness. I was only experiencing the proper "in-game death" I hadn't tasted since the beta test of *SAO*.

It was a strange feeling. All the color drained from my vision, leaving only a purplish monotone. Directly ahead there was a timer marked RESURRECTION COUNTDOWN in the same purple system font. Beyond that, I could see the silver guardians roaring happily at their victory and returning to the stained-glass windows on the ceiling of the dome.

There was no bodily sensation. I couldn't move, because the only thing left of me was the same tiny Remain Light that I'd seen from all the players I'd defeated so far. I felt lonely, small, pathetic.

That's right—it was miserable. But that was what I deserved for thinking, somewhere in the deepest parts of my brain, that this world was still only just a game. My strength was only in the numbers assigned to my character, but I'd acted like I could transcend the game, surpass its limits and do anything.

I wanted to see Asuna. I wanted to be held in her warm, healing embrace, and to set all of my thoughts and emotions free. But I couldn't reach her anymore.

The seconds ticked down. I couldn't remember what exactly would happen when the timer reached zero.

Whatever the case, there was only one thing I could do: crawl back to this place and challenge the guardians again. No matter how many times I lost, no matter if it was even possible or not, I'd keep doing it until the moment my very existence was permanently scraped out of this world for good...

It was then that a shadow glinted across my vision, which was pointed straight downward.

Someone had come through the still-open entrance and was racing upward at astonishing speed. I tried to shout at them not to come, but of course, there was no sound. I looked upward to see the guardian knights dripping out of those windows again.

The white giants passed right by me, screeching in that skin-crawling way, bearing down on the intruder. I'd just learned from experience that they were too much to tackle alone. I prayed the person would run away, but my would-be rescuer was making a beeline straight for me.

Several of the frontmost guardians swung their enormous blades downward. The intruder nimbly darted away, but one of the delayed swings found purchase. Even that mere graze sent the fragile challenger tumbling away.

But the intruder used that momentum to speed even faster around the line of knights and onward. As the figure grew closer, the number of guardians protecting the dome grew and grew, thick in the air, their screeches echoing.

The attacker swung a long katana but used it only for defense, guiding the enemy into clumps and using them as a barrier to avoid attack from afar. The valiant flight of the mystery invader was touching, and more than a little painful to watch.

Once within range, I heard a passionate, teary-eyed scream.

"Kirito!!"

It was Leafa. The sylph reached out with both hands and enveloped me.

We were already close to the gate, and the knights crowded the space above to block us out, a multilayered wall of flesh. But once Leafa had me safe and sound, she turned and sped back downward toward the exit.

The chanting of a spell echoed forth from behind us, and promptly a hailstorm of bright arrows roared past. Leafa spun right and left, trying to evade the projectiles, but they were as thick as monsoon rain, and I felt the vibration of each one that landed.

"*Hrg!!*"

Leafa held her breath but did not slow her descent. The arrows *thud*ded heavily into her, and I could see her HP bar fall below half. But the follow-up was not just arrows of light: Two guardian knights closed in from either side, their swords crossed at right angles.

She took evasive maneuvers via a right-hand tailspin, and successfully avoided one of the blades. But the other massive metal bludgeon caught her square on the back.

"Ah…"

Leafa was tossed as easily as a ball and slammed into the approaching ground. After several bracing bounces, she slid across the floor and came to a hard stop. Several of the guardians descended to the ground to finish her off.

She propped herself up with a hand and beat her wings once. That was enough to roll her across the ground—and suddenly my vision was full of bright sunlight. We were outside the dome.

———

Leafa threw her body against the cobblestones and panted heavily, chilled with fear. Somehow, despite the desperate odds, they'd made it out. She looked back to see the giant stone doors beginning to close and the white giants leaping back up to their dome. The event's timer must have run out.

There was a small, rippling black flame in her arms. She wanted to cradle Kirito, to whisper reassurances, but now was not the time for indulging in emotion. She sat up and crawled over to the stone statue nearby, resting her back against its feet as she waved a hand and opened her menu.

Leafa hadn't mastered water and holy magic yet, so she couldn't cast the high-level resurrection spell. Her only option was to extract a small blue bottle called "Dew of the World Tree."

She closed the window and popped the cap on the bottle, pouring the sparkling liquid onto Kirito's Remain Light. A three-dimensional magic sigil very similar to that of a resurrection spell formed, and a few seconds later, the familiar shape of the spriggan reappeared.

"...Kirito," she called out tearfully, still sitting down. Kirito returned a sad smile of his own, knelt on the stones, and put his hand on top of Leafa's.

"Thank you, Leafa. But please don't push yourself like that for my sake. I'll be fine...I don't want to put you through any more trouble."

"Trouble? No..."

She wanted to explain to him that it wasn't like that, but he was on his feet already. He spun around—and headed right back toward the door into the World Tree.

"K-Kirito!" Leafa called out, shocked. Somehow, she got her trembling legs upright. "W-wait...You can't go alone!"

"You might be right...But I have to do it anyway..." he murmured, his back turned. Leafa felt like a glass statue bearing its absolute weight limit. She desperately sought the right words, but her throat felt burned; no voice would emerge. She reached out at the last moment and grabbed him tight.

She could tell that she was drawn to him. Perhaps this was just an escape, a different route for her feelings for Kazuto, but at the same time, she didn't mind that. She knew this feeling was true.

"Please...don't...Come back to the old Kirito...I...I want to tell you something..."

Kirito enveloped the hand that was holding him. His soft but firm voice flowed into her ears.

"I'm sorry, Leafa…If I don't go there, nothing is over, and nothing can begin. I have to see her one more time…"

"I have…to see Asuna again."

For a moment, she didn't understand what she'd heard. The echo of his words rattled around in the blank space they'd created in her mind.

"…What…what did…you say…?"

He repeated himself, looking a bit curious.

"Oh…Asuna? That's the name of the person I'm looking for."

"But…but she's—"

Leafa faltered a step, her hands on her mouth.

Images were blotting their way into her frozen brain.

Kazuto in the dojo after their sparring a few days ago.

Kirito's defeat of the salamanders in the Ancient Forest—their first meeting.

Both boys would swipe their swords to the right at the end of their fights and put them over their backs. The images aligned perfectly.

The two silhouettes melted into a spray of light. Leafa opened her eyes wide, the words barely escaping her trembling lips.

"…Big…Brother…?"

"Huh…?"

Kirito's brows suddenly knotted in suspicion. His jet-black eyes stared straight into Leafa's. The light in his pupils rippled, quavered, like a reflection of the moon in water.

"Sugu…? Suguha?"

The spriggan's voice was barely a whisper.

Leafa took several more faltering steps backward. The cobblestones, the town, the World Tree, the very universe around her— all seemed to be collapsing.

Over the last few days of adventuring with her new friend,

Leafa had felt color and life return to this virtual world. Just flying next to him sent her heart leaping.

She'd be lying if she claimed that loving Kazuto as Suguha and being attracted to Kirito as Leafa didn't fill her with guilt. But it was Kirito who had taught her that the world of Alfheim didn't have to be just an extension of a virtual flight simulator, but another true reality. Because of that, Leafa had realized that the feelings she felt here were true, not just digital data.

She thought that maybe she could freeze the heart that beat for Kazuto, bury it deeply, and eventually forget that pain by being with Kirito. But now the human being who gave the fairy character life, the one who helped make this world its own reality, had come into a very sharp and unexpected clarity.

"...This can't be happening...This is so wrong," Leafa wailed to herself, shaking her head. She couldn't stand to be here for a second longer. She had to turn away and open her menu.

There was no need to even look at the button in the bottom-left corner of her window, or the confirmation prompt it created. Eyes closed, she passed through the ring of rainbow light and was soon plunged into darkness.

When she woke up in her own bed, the first thing she saw was the deep blue of Alfheim's sky. The color that had always filled her with longing and nostalgia now caused her nothing but pain.

Suguha slowly pulled off the AmuSphere and held it in front of her.

"*Hih...huu...*"

The sobs came pouring from her throat. Her hands impulsively clenched the fragile device, no more than two thin circles of plastic. It began to bend, creaking faintly with the pressure.

She almost wanted to break the AmuSphere, to permanently sever her pathway to that other world—but she couldn't. She felt too sorry for Leafa, the girl living on the other side of the ring.

Suguha put the device on top of the bed and sat up. She put her feet on the floor, closed her eyes, and hung her head. She just didn't want to think about anything.

A quiet knock on the door broke the silence. It was followed by a voice with the same inflection, though different from Kirito's.

"Can I come in, Sugu?"

"No! Don't open the door!" she shouted abruptly. "Just…let me be alone…"

"What's wrong, Sugu? I mean, I was sure surprised, too…" he continued, clearly confused. "If you're mad that I was using the NerveGear again, I apologize. But I had to do it."

"No, it's not that."

She couldn't stop the current of emotion from tearing through her. Suguha leaped to her feet and strode to the door. She turned the knob and pulled, and there was Kazuto. He looked at her with obvious concern.

"I…I…" Her feelings turned into tears and tears into words before she could stop them. "I-I betrayed my own heart. I betrayed my love for you."

At last she had spoken the word *love* to his face, but it slashed her chest, her throat, her lips, like a knife. The pain seared at her, but she kept going.

"I was going to forget, to give up, to fall in love with Kirito. In fact, I already had. And yet…and yet…"

"Huh…?"

For several seconds he gaped at her silently. Then he whispered, "You love…? But…we're…"

"I know."

"…Huh…?"

"I already know."

Oh no, she thought. But she couldn't stop. She put all of her raging emotions into her stare and pushed on, lips trembling.

"We aren't real siblings. I've known that for over two years!!"

No. Suguha hadn't asked her mother to hold back on revealing that she knew the truth to Kazuto just so that she could hurl her feelings at him like this. She wanted time to properly consider what it meant, and what she could do about it.

"When you quit practicing kendo and started avoiding me years ago, it was because you learned the truth, wasn't it? You were keeping your distance because you knew I wasn't your real sister. So why have you decided to be nice to me now?!"

No matter how much she knew she ought to stop, she couldn't. As Suguha's words echoed through the cold hallway, Kazuto's black eyes gradually lost their expression.

"I...I was so happy when you came back from *SAO*. I was so happy when you started treating me the way you used to. I thought you finally saw me for who I was."

At last, two teardrops hit her cheeks. She rubbed at them fiercely and strained to push the voice from her lungs.

"But...after this, I'd rather you kept being cold to me. Then I wouldn't have realized that I love you...I wouldn't have been sad to learn about Asuna...and I wouldn't have fallen in love with Kirito to replace you!!"

Kazuto's eyes grew just a bit wider, and then his expression froze. After several seconds in which everything seemed to have stopped, his eyes wavered, then looked down. A single word came from his mouth.

"...Sorry..."

In the two months since he'd awakened, Kazuto's eyes had always been full of a tender, gentle light when he looked at Suguha. Now that light was gone, and a deep darkness had taken its place. Suguha felt sharp regret pierce her chest as painfully as any blade.

"...Just leave me alone."

She couldn't stand to look at him any longer. Suguha slammed the door to escape the guilt and self-loathing that threatened to crush her. She stumbled back several steps until her heel hit the bed, and she fell over onto it.

Suguha curled up into a ball on top of the sheets, her shoulders shaking with the force of her sobs. The tears poured forth, leaving small blots on the white sheets as they soaked into the fabric.

I stood for a long moment in front of the shut door. Eventually I turned around, leaned back against it, and slid down to a sitting position.

Suguha's suspicion that I'd been keeping my distance because she wasn't my real sister was basically correct. But I was only ten when I'd noticed the blank field in the census data and asked my parents what it meant. But there hadn't been a direct intention behind my estrangement with her.

That was the point when I'd lost my perspective of personal distance with *everyone*, not just Suguha.

I had no memories of my actual parents, and Minetake and Midori Kirigaya had loved me exactly the same both before and after I knew the truth, so it wasn't an external shock to my system. Instead, the event planted the seed of a very odd sensation deep inside of me, where it took root.

It was a kind of suspicion, a constant question in every interaction: Who is this person, really? No matter how long I'd known them, no matter how well I knew them—even my own family members—I couldn't prevent that thought from running through my brain: Who is this person, exactly? Do I really know them?

Perhaps that was one thing that drove me to the world of online games. On the Net, it was natural for every character to have a secret inner side. No one really knew anyone. Interacting in this world of falsehood where that was taken for granted just seemed comfortable to me. I plunged headfirst into Net gaming around fifth or sixth grade, and never looked back. It would eventually take me into a world that I wouldn't escape for an entire two years.

If it weren't for the whole "game of death" thing, *Sword Art Online* could have been my paradise. A world of false dreams from which I'd never wake. An unending virtual realm.

I tried to play the role of Kirito, just an unfamiliar nobody.

But being trapped in that full-dive experience and unable to escape eventually led me to one pure truth:

The real world and the false world were ultimately the same thing.

Human beings only recognized the world based on the information their brains received. The only thing that made an online game a "false" world was that it could be left behind with the simple flip of a switch.

SAO was a world that my brain recognized with electronic pulses, and a world that couldn't be escaped.

And that description matched the real world perfectly.

Once I had that epiphany, I understood how empty the doubts that had plagued me since the age of ten really were. There was no meaning to wondering who anyone really was. All you could do was trust and accept them. The people you knew really were the people you knew.

I could hear the faint sound of Suguha sobbing through the door.

When I first saw her face after returning alive from *SAO*, I was openly and honestly happy to see her again. I knew that in order to make up for the years of distance that my pointless issue had caused, I'd need to close the gap by treating her the way I truly wanted.

But it seemed that over those two years, Suguha had discovered her own truth about me. She'd learned that I was her cousin, not her brother, and the shift in the distance she felt was surely alarming and strange to her, a challenge to accept. And, assuming that she didn't know the truth, I'd been totally unaware of what was happening to her.

I'd revealed my feelings toward Asuna on multiple occasions in Suguha's presence. I'd even cried over Asuna in front of her. I could never have imagined that it was hurting her so much to hear that.

And that wasn't all.

Suguha had never been one for computers and video games. It

must have been because of me that she'd started on a VRMMO of her own. Suguha had spent countless hours diving into that virtual world, trying to know more about me, creating another version of herself. Leafa, the girl who'd helped me time and time again in Alfheim...was Suguha.

Yui had said the reason I ran into her first thing after logging in was possibly due to another person in the vicinity being logged in to *ALO*. It wasn't just the local vicinity, it was from the same damn house; our global IP was the same. Leafa and I had been fated to meet this way, but even as Kirito, I couldn't think of anyone but Asuna, and I hurt Leafa just like I hurt Suguha.

I squeezed my eyes shut and opened them so hard it was practically audible, then jumped vigorously to my feet.

Now was the time to do something for Suguha. If there was one thing the people of *SAO* had taught me, it was to reach out when words weren't enough.

—◊◊—

The loud knock jolted Suguha out of her detached haze, and she hunched tighter in response.

She wanted to shout out not to open the door, but the only thing that left her throat was ragged breath. But Kazuto didn't turn the knob—he spoke through the door.

"Sugu...I'll be waiting on the northern terrace of Alne."

His voice was calm and gentle. She could sense him leaving her door. Farther down the hallway, the door to his room opened and shut, and silence descended.

Suguha shut her eyes tight and hunched up again. The tears that squeezed out made little *plips* as they hit the floor.

There was no shock or agitation in Kazuto's voice. After all the hurtful things she'd said to him, he must have internalized it.

He's so strong. I can't be like him...

She thought of that painful night several days ago. Like Suguha now, Kazuto had been curled up on his bed. Just like her, he'd been crying for the sake of someone he couldn't reach. He'd been like a helpless child with no solution to his problem.

The next day, she'd met Kirito. That meant that Kazuto had somehow found information that his sleeping beloved was in *ALfheim Online*—on the top of the World Tree—and thrown himself into that quest. He'd wiped his tears aside and grabbed his sword.

And I told him to hang in there. Not to give up. And yet here I am, still crying…

Suguha slowly opened her eyes. There was a shining crown ahead of her.

She reached out, lifted it, and set it on her head.

The pale sunlight falling through the wispy clouds seemed to soften the ancient stone architecture of Alne.

Kirito was not at the log-in location. She checked the map to see that the entrance to the dome was on the south end of the World Tree, while the north side featured a large terrace for events. He would be waiting for her there.

Now that she'd come this far, she was afraid to see him. She didn't know what she ought to say, and had no idea what he might tell her. Leafa took a few dejected steps forward and sat on a bench to the side of the square.

How many minutes did she spend looking at the ground? There was a sensation of someone landing nearby, and Leafa froze, shutting her eyes.

But the person who called her name was not who she expected.

"Arrrgh, I was looking all over for you, Leafa!"

Despite the whiny tinge to the voice, it was energetic and familiar. She looked up with a start to see a sylph with greenish-blond hair.

"R-Recon?!"

The emergence of this surprising face made her forget the pain for a moment. When asked why he was there, Recon put his hands on his hips and bent over confidently.

"Well, I noticed that Sigurd had left the sewer, so when my paralysis wore off, I took my shot and poisoned both of the salamanders dead. Then I went off to find him and make *him* taste some poison, but he was no longer in sylph territory, so I decided to just head for Alne myself, and the only way to get through the mountains was to keep drawing aggro from all the monsters and foist the trains off on other people until I made it here this morning. It took all night!"

"So you're saying... you PKed people with monsters...?"

"Look, don't sweat the fine details!"

Recon excitedly plopped down next to Leafa, totally unconcerned with her observation. Then he must have realized that she was alone, and looked around curiously.

"Where's that spriggan? Did you split up already?"

"Well..."

Leafa chose her words carefully, inching away to put more space between them. Despite the diversion, there was still a lump of pain in her chest, and no convenient excuse came to mind. The next thing she knew, she was baring it all.

"I...I said some awful things to him...I love him, but I said such hurtful things. I'm an idiot..."

The tears nearly came flooding out again, but Leafa kept them in. Shinichi Nagata was her classmate in real life, and this was only a virtual world, so she didn't want to burden him with a flood of raw emotion. She turned away and spoke quickly.

"I'm sorry for being weird. Forget about it. I'm not going to see him anymore...so let's just go back to Swilvane..."

No matter how hard she tried to run, in reality they were only a matter of feet away from each other. But Leafa was still afraid to see Kirito. She decided she'd ignore his summons, go back to Swilvane, greet the few people she liked there, then let Leafa go into a long hibernation. At least until her pain had faded.

Her mind made up, Leafa looked over at Recon, then abruptly flinched backward.

"Wh...what?!"

Recon's face was as red and puffy as if it had been boiled. His eyes bulged and his mouth worked soundlessly. For a moment she forgot they were safe in town, and thought he might have been hit with a suffocation spell. Recon suddenly darted forward to grab her hands and held them to his chest.

"Wh-wh-what's happening?!"

"Leafa!" he shouted, so loudly that other players were turning to look. He leaned over Leafa and stared into her eyes, despite her best efforts to pull back as far as possible.

"Y-you shouldn't cry! You're not Leafa if you're not smiling all the time! I...I'll always be with you, in real life or in the game... L-L-Leafa—I mean, Suguha...I l-love you!"

The words poured out of him as though he were a broken faucet. Rather than wait for her answer, he shoved his face even closer. There was a mad gleam in his normally weak eyes, and his nostrils were flared wide as his lips closed in on her.

"U-um, hang on..."

Ambushes were Recon's specialty in battle, but this was beyond even that. Leafa couldn't move for the shock that possessed her body. Recon must have taken that for assent, and loomed even closer, his body practically covering hers.

"W-wait...stop..."

When he was close enough that she could feel the warmth breath of his nostrils, Leafa's stun effect finally wore off, and she clenched a fist.

"I told you...to stop it!!" She tensed and delivered a short but powerful blow to his solar plexus.

"*Gwufh!!*"

There was no damaging other players in the safe zone of town, but there was still a knock-back effect. Recon flew several feet into the air and crashed down onto a bench. He held his stomach, writhing in agony.

"Hrrrgh...Th-that was messed up, Leafa..."

"Which part?! Learn to control yourself, you dingus!" she ranted, finally feeling her face flush. The rage and shame of almost having been kissed roared within her like dragon breath. She grabbed Recon by the collar and gave him a few more good punches with her other hand.

"Geh! Agh! O-okay, okay, I'm sorry!!"

He fell off the bench and propped himself up on the paving stones with his right hand, shaking his head frantically. When Leafa relaxed her attacking stance, he sat up, cross-legged, and hung his head.

"Dang it...It doesn't make sense...I thought it was just a matter of me having the guts to go ahead and tell you..."

"You..." she sighed, "are an idiot."

"Aww..."

He looked like a scolded puppy dog. It was such a ridiculous expression that Leafa passed straight over exasperation into laughter. She let out a deep breath, half sigh and half giggle. Her heart felt as though some of the weight had left it.

Leafa suddenly wondered if she'd been internalizing everything a bit too much. She'd been gritting her teeth the entire time, afraid of being hurt. Because of that constant backward pressure, when the dam broke all those feelings poured out in a flood. She'd hurt someone very important to her.

It might be too late—but she at least wanted to be honest to herself. Once she realized this, the tension went out of her shoulders. She looked up and murmured, "But that's the part about you that I don't mind."

"Huh? R-really?!"

Recon hopped up on the bench again and grabbed Leafa's hand—no lesson learned.

"Don't get cocky, buster!" She slipped out of his grasp and floated up into the air.

"I'm going to follow your example from time to time. I need you to wait here, though. And if you actually trail me, you'll get worse than this!" She brandished her fist menacingly under Recon's shocked face, then spun around, beat her wings, and flew up toward the trunk of the World Tree.

After several minutes of flying around the frighteningly massive tree, a wide terrace came into view below. The space was apparently used for flea markets and guild events, but it was empty today. There was little else on the north side of Alne, so there weren't even any tourists wandering by.

A small black figure waited at the center of the wide-open space. It had sharply angled gray wings, and a massive sword slung diagonally between them.

Leafa took a deep breath, collecting her nerves, and descended to him.

"...Hey."

Kirito gave her an easy grin, though there was some tension behind it.

"Thanks for waiting," she replied. Silence followed. The only sound between them was the whistling of the wind blowing past.

"Sugu," Kirito eventually said. His eyes were shining with serious intent, but Leafa cut him off with the wave of a hand. She beat her wings and took a step back.

"Let's have a duel, Big Brother. To finish the one we started the other day."

She put a hand on her katana and his eyes went wide. He opened his mouth briefly, then shut it.

Kirito's dark eyes stared at her, the deep glimmer the only feature he shared with his real-life counterpart, and he eventually nodded. He flapped his wings and stepped back.

"All right. No handicaps this time," he said, still grinning, and put his hand on his sword hilt.

They drew at the same time, the clear, crips sounds overlapping. Leafa held her familiar blade dead still at medium height, staring at Kirito. He lowered his stance, just barely keeping the giant sword off the ground. Just as he had the other day.

"You don't have to hold back at the last second. Here goes!!"

They leaped forward as one.

In the instant they closed the gap, Leafa had an epiphany. That stance of his she'd thought so preposterous during their duel must have been perfected in this virtual world. After all, he'd spent every day of those two years fighting for his life.

For the first time, she wanted to know. Wanted to know what he'd seen, what he'd felt, and how he'd lived in that other world, that death game that had never been anything but the target of her hatred.

Leafa brought her katana straight down from overhead. In Swilvane they'd said her slashes were unavoidable, but Kirito evaded it with just the slightest of motions. His greatsword came howling up at her. She brought the katana forward to deflect it, but the heavy shock left her hands numb.

They each used the backward momentum of the deflection to leap. Beating their wings, they became two opposing spirals, traveling upward to strike again in midair. There was an explosion of light and sound, and the earth shook.

As both a fairy warrior and a kendo athlete, Leafa had to admire Kirito's ability. He was equally adept at both offense and defense, as smooth and beautiful as a dance. The longer she matched his rhythm of strikes and sways, the more Leafa felt that she was ascending to new heights she'd never experienced before. None of the duels she'd ever taken part in here had ever truly satisfied her. She'd lost before, but it was always due to some special quality of the opponent's weapon, or a spell. No one had bested Leafa through sword skill alone.

Now that she'd finally found someone who was even better, and he was her beloved, Leafa was filled with something like joy. Even if they never shared their hearts again, this special moment was enough for her. In time, she noticed that there were tears pooling in her eyes.

After several bracing clashes, Leafa let the momentum push

her into a backward leap for some distance. She spread her wings wide to come to a halt, and raised her katana high, high over her head.

Kirito seemed to understand that this would be her final attack. He twisted, notching his sword even farther back.

For a moment, all was as still as the surface of a pond on a windless day.

The tears fell down Leafa's cheeks without a sound, dripping off her chin and sending ripples through the silence. They moved together.

She raced downward, as if to set the air on fire. Her long katana traced an arc of pure light. Kirito was dashing up to meet her head-on. His sword also burned white, cutting the air in two.

Just as her beloved's blade passed by her head, Leafa let go.

The masterless sword flew forward, an arrow of light. But she did not follow it with her eyes. She spread her arms wide, ready to embrace Kirito's blade.

She knew this would not satisfy him. But she didn't have the right words to apologize for the foolishness of her hurtful statement.

So this was her means of making amends: She'd offer this other version of herself to his sword.

Arms wide and eyes half-closed, Leafa waited for the moment to come.

But as her vision melted into white, Kirito flew toward her, his hands—empty.

"…?!"

She went wide-eyed. In the corner of her vision, she noticed that, like hers, his sword was spinning off through open air. He'd discarded his own weapon at the same moment she'd thrown hers.

Before she had time to ask herself why, they crossed in mid-air. Kirito collided with her, his arms also open wide. The impact knocked the breath from her lungs, and all she could do was cling to him.

Unable to cancel out the momentum, their bodies spun off through the air. The world turned into a blurry smear of blue sky and brown tree.

"Why would—" It was all she could manage get out, somehow.

At the same time, staring into her face from just inches away, he said, "Why did—"

They both fell silent and let inertia carry them through the Alfheim sky, staring deeply into each other's eyes. After a while, Kirito spread his wings to catch the air and slow their rotation.

"I-I wanted to apologize, Sugu. But...I didn't have the right words...so I was going to let you hit me instead..."

She suddenly felt Kirito's arms tighten around her back.

"I'm so sorry, Sugu. After all that time away...I haven't been seeing you for who you are. I've been so wrapped up in my own affairs that I didn't try to hear what you were really saying. I'm sorry..."

The tears poured out of Leafa's eyes as she in took his words.

"No...I'm the one who..."

But she couldn't continue. Leafa sobbed audibly, burying her face in his chest.

She was still thinking she wanted the moment to continue forever when the two of them came to a soft landing on the grass. Kirito continued stroking her head as she sobbed and hiccupped, but a few minutes later, he began to speak in hushed tones.

"To tell you the truth...I still haven't really come back from there. It's not over yet. My real life won't start again until she wakes up...so I still don't know what to think about you, Sugu..."

"...Okay," she murmured, nodding. "I'll be waiting. Waiting for the moment you truly do come back to our home. I'm here to help. Tell me...about her. And how it was you came to this game..."

8

After they recovered the two discarded swords, Kirito and Leafa flew back to the landing before the guardian statues at the tree gate. To Leafa's surprise, Recon had been obediently waiting there. His face ran through a blinding series of emotions upon seeing the black-clad spriggan next to her until, finally, he inquired, "So...how did it go?"

Leafa beamed and said, "We're going to conquer the World Tree. Me, you, and him."

"Oh...Wait—what?!"

He faltered backward, face pale. She patted him on the shoulder, wished him luck, and turned to look at the massive stone doors. They seemed to be emitting a freezing chill to intimidate all comers.

However, after having seen a warrior as great as Kirito mercilessly crushed by those guardian knights not long ago, Leafa didn't think that adding two more to the party would make a difference. She looked over and saw that Kirito was biting his lip, his face tense.

But suddenly he looked up, as though pondering a sudden idea. "You there, Yui?"

Before the words had finished coming out of his mouth, a light coalesced in midair and the familiar pixie was there. She put her hands on her hips and pouted, clearly furious.

"What took you so long? I can't appear until you call me, Papa!"

"Sorry, sorry. Things were busy."

He grinned apologetically and offered his palm to the pixie, who sat down on it. In a flash, Recon craned his neck over to examine her with rabid curiosity.

"W-wow, is this a Private Pixie?! I've never seen one before! Holy cow, she's so cute!!"

Yui pulled back in concern, eyes wide. "Wh-who is this person?!"

"Come on, you're scaring her," Leafa scolded Recon, pulling him away by the ear. "You don't have to worry about him, he's not dangerous."

"Um... okay," Kirito said, blinking in surprise. He turned back to Yui. "So, did you learn anything from that battle?"

"Yes," she replied, an adorably serious look on her little face. "Those guardian monsters aren't all that impressive in terms of stats—it's their appearance patterns that are dangerous. The closer to the gate you got, the faster they spawned. At the closest point, they were appearing twelve per second. I can only assume it was designed to be impossible..."

"Hmm." Kirito nodded, his face severe. "You wouldn't notice because each individual guardian goes down in a hit or two, but as a total, they add up to an unbeatable, titanic boss. They're going to tantalize the player base and make it virtually impossible, but just easy enough to keep them interested. That'll make this very tough..."

"But, Papa, your skill levels are also off the charts. With your instantaneous bursts of strength, it might be possible."

"..."

Kirito lapsed into silence again, then looked at last to Leafa.

"I'm sorry. Can I ask you to indulge me one last time? I know it would be easier to find more people or search for another way, rather than attempting this madness again. But... I just have a bad feeling. Like we're running out of time..."

His suggestion gave Leafa the momentary idea to send a message to the Lord's Mansion in Swilvane. Lady Sakuya might be able to send the highest-level sylphs to assist their battle.

But she bit her lip and quickly abandoned the idea. The image of the undine party down in Jotunheim early that morning flooded into her mind. They'd tried to hunt an unresisting Deviant God against Leafa's pleas, prioritizing efficiency and safety.

Her friend Sakuya would not think the same way as the undines, of course. But she was the leader of their people and bore great responsibility. Her position demanded commonsense decisions for the sake of the entire race. Even if they did eventually make an attempt on the World Tree, it would only be after ample preparations. They would not fly out en masse, prepped for the slaughter, on Leafa's request alone.

After a brief silence, she looked up and stated clearly, "All right. Let's try it one more time. I'll do anything I can to help...and so will he."

"Awww..."

She elbowed Recon in the ribs and he exhibited his very best droopy-eyebrowed whimper. But he grudgingly admitted that he and Leafa were of one body and mind, nodding in resignation.

The stone doors opened with a rumbling that seemed to issue from the very center of the earth. Leafa's wings trembled slightly at the eerie aura that seemed to flow from the space beyond. She'd been in a blind haste when racing after Kirito earlier, but standing in front of it now, she had to admit there was a palpable feeling of pressure exuding from the place.

But on the inside, she was surprisingly calm.

She was in the eye of the storm. Both here and in the real world, everything was loudly and alarmingly changing around her. She had no idea where it was all taking her. All she could do was fly, to the best of her ability, toward the light on the horizon.

Kirito, Leafa, and Recon drew their blades. Along with Yui, four pairs of eyes examined one another. Wings were spread.

"…Let's go!!"

Kirito signaled the charge, and they rose as one, flying into the dome.

Their plan called for Kirito to begin racing upward as fast as he could toward the gate in the center of the dome. Leafa and Recon would remain near the floor and ready their healing spells.

She could see the glowing surfaces on the ceiling begin to drip downward into gigantic white shapes. They bore down on Kirito, screeching in that horrible way. When the first wave of knights met the now-tiny spriggan in midair, a rumbling blast of light shook the dome.

Upon seeing several of the giants fall to pieces, split through the torso, Recon murmured, "…Wow."

The force of his blade was indeed formidable. But the sight of what was happening beyond Kirito's mad dash sent chills throughout Leafa's body.

There were just too many of them. The sheer density of the forces pouring out of the latticed ceiling was beyond any scale of game balance. Even the dungeons in Jotunheim, the most diabolical zone in all of *ALO*, wouldn't feature spawn rates anywhere near this pace.

The guardian knights bunched up into packs and dashed themselves against Kirito in roiling waves. Each collision resulted in a bright flash, after which the large white bodies would fall to pieces like snow. But for every one vanquished, three more appeared.

When he was halfway to the gate, Kirito had lost about 10 percent of his hit points. Leafa and Recon didn't miss a beat in unleashing the healing magic they'd kept stored for that moment. Blue light surrounded Kirito's body, and his gauge began to refill.

But when the spell reached him, something terrible happened.

The lowest-flying pack of guardian knights screeched in unison and turned toward *them*.

"Aaah…" Recon gasped in panic.

Leafa could feel the gaze behind their mirror masks directed at her. She clenched her teeth.

Leafa and Recon agreed not to target Kirito with anything other than healing spells to minimize the notice they might draw. Normally, monsters didn't pounce unless a player moved into their response zone, or attacked them with ranged weapons or spells.

But these guardians ran on a different algorithm than the monsters outside, one more dangerous and pernicious. If they could target even players casting support spells, then the orthodox system—attackers in the front, healers in the back—meant nothing.

The half-dozen knights ignored Leafa's silent plea to buzz off and descended on multiple pairs of wings. They carried enormous swords, each easily taller than her, that glinted with a hungry light.

She turned to Recon and shouted, "I'll draw them away—just keep healing!"

And without waiting for an answer, she made to rise. But Recon, who had always obeyed her commands in battle, grabbed her hand. When she turned around in shock, his voice was trembling, but his eyes were hard.

"Leafa...I don't understand everything that's going on here, but it's important to you, right?"

"That's right. This time, it's not just a game."

"I don't think I can match up to that spriggan...but I'll find a way to deal with those guardians."

Recon leaped into the air, controller stick in his hand. And as Leafa watched, dumbfounded, he flew off, charging directly into the swarm of knights.

"Y-you idiot..."

They were far beyond his ability, but it was too late for her to make up the distance by now. Meanwhile, across the dome, Kirito's HP bar was inching back down from its formerly full position. Leafa had no choice but to start chanting a healing spell. Even as she spoke the familiar words, she couldn't help but keep a nervous eye on Recon.

Recon unleashed the area-effect wind spell he'd been saving directly into the cloud of guardian knights. Multiple green blades fanned out and sliced through the onrushing knights. Their HP bars hardly took a dent, but it did have the effect of drawing all of their attention to him.

The white giants roared with distorted voices and closed in on the tiny green speck that dared to challenge them. Recon swished and darted like a leaf blown in a gale, just barely retreating out of the range of their swings. They raced after him.

Leafa finished casting and hurled her spell at Kirito, who was fighting far above. Again, it drew the notice of several guardians, who descended after her. This fresh group merged with the swarm following Recon, growing the white cloud to twice its size.

Recon had never been an expert at air battles, but he showed considerable concentration in evading the onslaught of swords. The occasional sword tip clipped his body, but no critical blows had swallowed up his HP yet.

"...Recon..."

Leafa was struck by the desperate effort of his flight, but it clearly would not last forever. Each time she cast a healing spell on Kirito, the number of knights descending on them grew.

Eventually, the pursuing guardians split into two groups and prepared to execute a pincer attack on Recon. One among the rain of blows caught him square in the back, smashing him through the air.

"That's enough, Recon! Flee to the outside!" she screamed, unable to watch anymore. As long as the battle still raged inside, anyone who left the arena could not return. She'd just have to do her best to hold them off. Leafa took to the air, preparing another healing spell.

But at that moment, Recon turned back to her. Leafa's wings stopped when she saw the purposeful smile on his face.

Despite the many sword blows, Recon began casting a new spell. His body glowed with a deep purple light.

"...?!"

Leafa held her breath, realizing that it was the shine of dark magic. A complex magical sigil began to form in midair, and based on its size, it must have been a high-level spell. Dark magic was so rare around sylph lands that she had no idea what effect this one might have.

The sigil unfolded again and again, growing ever larger, until it finally engulfed all of the attacking knights. For an instant, the complex runes and figures contracted—then shone with an overwhelming light.

"Ah—!!"

Leafa had to turn her face from the blinding glow. An explosion so great it sounded like the earth splitting apart shot through the entire dome.

It took a full second for her eyesight to recover from pure white. Leafa looked toward the center of the explosion with her hands up for shielding, and what she saw left her speechless. The entire pack of tightly clustered knights was gone without a trace. Only a few wisps of purple light remained.

It was an unbelievable blast. There were no wind-magic area spells that powerful—not even any fire spells. Leafa cheered even as she wondered how Recon had acquired this incredible ace up his sleeve. A few more of those, and they might just be able to reach the gate after all. She prepared to cast a healing spell on him—and froze again.

Recon was nowhere to be seen in the last remnants of the explosion. There was only a tiny green Remain Light floating in the air.

"A...self-destruct spell...?" she wondered aloud. But then she remembered once hearing about such a dark magic spell long ago. It was practically a forbidden art—in exchange for its power, the ordinary death penalty was several times worse.

After a few moments of silence, Leafa shut her eyes tight. It was just a game, just experience points, but the effort and intent Recon had expended for their sake was true sacrifice. They could not retreat now. She opened her eyes again and looked up.

What she saw turned her legs to jelly.

The ceiling of the dome was now one entire mass of squirming, teeming white shapes.

The tiny black dot that was Kirito was close, so close to the top. With each flash of his sword, more knights fell to pieces, but it was like trying to dig a hole in a massive sand dune with but a needle. The wall of white flesh would give way for a brief moment, only to be filled just as quickly.

"*Raaahhh!!*"

Leafa could just barely hear Kirito's bloodcurdling roar. She raised her hands to cast a healing spell, but let them drop almost immediately.

"We can't, Big Brother...It's just too much..."

To be honest, she'd never taken Kirito's story about Asuna's soul being trapped in this game at face value. This was a game, a world to be enjoyed. Her brain couldn't help but reject the idea that this wonderful place shared anything in common with the nightmare of *SAO*.

But now, for the first time, Leafa began to sense a kind of malice within the system. Some unseen force, which was supposedly keeping everything in a fair balance, was wickedly, cruelly swinging a bloody scythe at the players' necks within this arena. There was no way to overcome this trap.

A low, twisted sound echoed throughout the dome like a chanted curse. Some of the guardian knights fell still, incanting a spell with their left arms extended. It was the Rain of Arrows spell that had stopped Kirito in his tracks the first time. The arrows caused enough of a stun effect for the sword blows to land next.

Leafa tensed up, imagining the sight of Kirito's body skewered by countless blades.

Suddenly, a roil of voices swept up from behind Leafa, over her vapid wings.

"Huh...?!"

She turned to see a party of sylph warriors, clad in gleaming new-green metal, pouring through the door in tight formation.

They were outfitted with full sets of what appeared to be ancient weapons, or something similar. Like a storm gust in the spring, they rushed past Leafa and headed straight for the dome's ceiling. There must have been at least fifty of them.

Stunned into silence, Leafa could only watch closely enough to call up their cursors as they passed. She couldn't see faces behind the heavy visors, but all the names that appeared on the cursors were the best of the best in sylph territory. Upon hearing their roar, the guardian knights preparing their spells stopped and began to shift tactics.

Leafa's back crawled with chills somewhere between excitement and overwhelming awe. But they were not the only ones coming to tackle the dome.

A few seconds after the last members of the sylph raid party came through the door, more shouts echoed through, accompanied by the thunderbolt roars of great beasts.

This new group was of much smaller number than the sylphs, perhaps ten in all. Individually, however, they were much larger.

"Dragons!" Leafa exclaimed.

It was a pack of dragons with gray scales, each the size of several players lined up head to foot. As proof that these creatures were not wild, the dragons were outfitted with gleaming golden armor on their foreheads, chests, and the fronts of their wings.

Pairs of silver chains extended from the head armor as reins, which the riders on the beasts's saddles gripped. These dragon knights had brand-new armor of their own, but there was no missing the triangular ears or the long, sinewy tails extending out the backs of their leggings.

These were dragoons, the ultimate fighting force of the cait siths. The legendary warriors were kept hidden from the public— there wasn't even a screenshot floating about on the Internet. But here they were, in the flesh.

Leafa's wings were at full extension, the very blood in her veins seeming to dance with elation. Suddenly, she heard someone call out from behind her.

"Sorry it took so long."

She turned around to see Lady Sakuya, leader of the sylphs, in her wooden geta sandals and kimono. Next to her was Lady Alicia Rue of the cait siths, whose ears flapped as she said, "So sorry. It took every member of the leprechaun blacksmith's guild until just now to finish up all the equipment and dragon armor. We spent all the money the spriggan gave us, plus all of our vault savings!"

"Meaning that if this fails, both of our races are bankrupt," Sakuya noted coolly, arms crossed.

They came. And so fast, knowing that both of them risked losing their prestigious positions. This joint force between two races so transcended the typical MMORPG battle over resources and risk management that surely even the game developers had never expected it to happen.

"Thank you...thank you both," Leafa said, her voice trembling. *There really are things in this world more important than rules and manners*, she told herself, heart soaring. There was nothing more to say.

Both leaders told her the time for thanks was later. They turned to survey the ceiling of the dome with severe skepticism. Sakuya loudly snapped her fan shut.

"Let us join the fray!"

All three nodded in agreement and leaped into the air. Above them, several groups of white guardians were dripping down from the ceiling to meet the charging sylph platoon. High in the center, Kirito was still locked in fierce battle, but he seemed to have noticed the cavalry's arrival, because he stopped attempting to rise for a moment, keeping his distance from the ceiling.

Alicia Rue flew directly to the center of the chamber and raised her hand, shouting in a clear (but precious) voice:

"Dragoons! Prepare breath attack!"

The ten dragon knights formed a wide, hovering circle around

the three of them. The dragons spread their wings wide and curved their necks into S shapes, orange flickers of fire visible behind their deadly fangs.

Next, Sakuya raised her lacquered fan.

"Sylphs, prepare your extra attacks!"

The tight pack of warriors held their swords overhead as they charged. The blades were enveloped by a lattice pattern of emerald-green light.

A large congregation of the guardian knights, so dense they resembled white maggots, descended upon them with hideous screeches. Alicia Rue waited for the creatures to get as close as possible, biting her lip with a long canine, then finally raised her hand and barked another order.

"Unleash fire breath!"

All ten dragons exhaled gouts of hellfire at once. Ten crimson pillars shot through the air, fanned out around the sylph warriors and Kirito, and blasted into the cloud of guardians.

A bright flash illuminated the dome. In the next moment, bulging fireballs exploded one after another, linking together into a tremendous wall of flame. The world was rocked with a massive roar. Guardian knights were blown to shreds by the force of the blast, adding their own little white flames as they burned away.

But the seemingly infinite wall of white simply formed another swarm that recklessly pushed its way through the flames. It fanned out wide like a spreading liquid, threatening to swallow Kirito whole.

Just before the blob of white could attack, Sakuya swung her fan down and shouted, "Unleash Fenrir Storm!!"

With perfect precision, the sylph platoon thrust their swords as one. Green lightning pulsed through fifty blades and then shot through the air to pierce the cloud of knights.

Everything was again awash in white light. There was no explosion this time, but instead thick bolts of ravenous lightning racing through the enemy, churning them to bits.

Twice decimated, the center part of the wall of guardian knights did indeed seem to be hollowing out. But like a liquid flowing back into shape, that depression was filling in from the sides.

This was their only chance, Leafa knew. She drew her long katana and darted forward. The two leaders had come to the same conclusion. Sakuya's voice cracked through the clearing like a whip.

"All units, charge!!"

It was undoubtedly the largest battle ever fought in Alfheim. The periodic bursts of fire breath from the rear set the guardians aflame and falling to the earth. The sylph party worked in perfect formation like a single projectile, gouging great holes in the wall of flesh with their wave of deadly swords.

Standing at the front of that projectile was the tiny black form of the spriggan. His equipment was clearly inferior to the sylphs', but the holy speed with which he whipped his giant sword around meant that anything coming into contact with him burst into smithereens.

Leafa raced through a small aperture in the center of the sylph formation to take position directly behind Kirito. She used her katana to deflect an attack bearing down on his back, plunging the long blade into the glowing white guardian beneath its mirrored mask. With a vigorous flip of her wrists, she knocked the head clean off. Its body burned with white flames.

Kirito took a look behind him and mouthed, *Sugu—watch my back!*

I've got you covered! she indicated with a glance, turning to stand back-to-back with him. They stayed that way, spinning round and round, slashing and hacking at the oncoming knights.

The giant guardians would not be so easy in a one-on-one fight. But standing next to Kirito and matching his speed, Leafa felt the enemy moving slower and slower. Or was her mind just working faster? It felt as though all of the stimuli from all of her senses were focused at one single point in the center of her brain. This was a sensation she'd only noticed a few times before, during kendo competitions.

It was as though she and Kirito were one. All of her nerves and brain cells were connected and racing with pale electronic pulses. She knew where Kirito was moving behind her without seeing him. As they spun together, Leafa struck the head off the guardian knight Kirito had been sparring with, while he sank his sword directly into the wound she'd made in the enemy she'd just left.

Kirito, Leafa, the sylphs, and the dragoons all formed one being of pure energy that melted, gouged, and burst through the limitless flood of knights. Though the enemy might be endless, the spatial limits of the dome were fixed. As long as they kept proceeding forward, their moment of victory would come.

"*Seyaaa!*" Leafa cried, splitting a guardian's body straight down the middle. For an instant, through its crumbling corpse, she saw the ceiling.

"Raah!"

Kirito broke away from Leafa's back and plunged through the gap in the wall of flesh like a bolt of black lightning. The last line of guardian knight defense roared with hatred and closed in on all sides. There were at least thirty of them.

"Kirito!!"

On pure instinct, Leafa pulled back her sword and hurled it with all her might at Kirito's left hand. The light green hilt of the spinning katana fit right into his palm, as though it were being pulled to it.

"Rraaaahh!!"

With a bellow that seemed to shake the entire dome, he alternated swipes of the blades, greatsword in his right hand and katana in his left.

A slash down from the right. A slice up from the left. The two shining swords traced slightly different angles each time, until they formed a glowing circle of white like that of the corona around a solar eclipse. The guardian knights were torn to ribbons by dozens of light-speed slashes, their remains littering the air.

Beyond the quivering ring of End Flames, she could see it clearly now. Right in the center of the vine-crossed ceiling of the

dome was the round door, split into four sections. The final gate of Alfheim, leading through the trunk of the World Tree to the palace seated at its crown.

The black figure left a trail of light as he raced for the gate. He was through at last.

Before Leafa's eyes, countless layers of guardian knights surged forward and buried the hole that had been there just an instant before. Sakuya had seen Kirito break through the line of defense and shouted an order:

"All units, turn back and disengage!"

Leafa joined the sylph squad and headed into a dive as the dragons' fire breath protected their backs. For an instant, she looked back at the ceiling. She couldn't see Kirito for the wall of guardians, but in her mind's eye, he flew higher, ever higher, toward the heights that no one had yet reached.

Fly—fly—fly as far as you can! Through the tree, through the sky, to the center of the world!

———

I closed the final distance so fast, I thought my brain cells would fry.

Before my eyes was the final round gate. Four stone slabs met in the center to form a cross shape. And beyond them—Asuna. Along with the half of my soul that had been left behind in that fateful realm.

From behind me came a scream of hatred from the guardian knights. I looked back, sensing their pursuit. There were fresh knights being born without end from the glowing apertures around the gate, and they flew down to intercept me.

But I was faster. I could reach out and touch the gate now.

And yet...

"It won't open!" I exclaimed with shock.

The gate would not open. I'd assumed the heavy, evil-looking door would simply slide open once I got close enough, but the intersecting cracks showed no signs of budging.

It was too late to slow down. I held my right sword at my side, preparing to smash my way through the stone wall if it came to that.

The next instant, I slammed into the gate with astonishing force. The tip of the sword sent sparks flying with the impact, but there wasn't the slightest sign of a scratch on the stone surface.

"Yui, what's going on?!" I screamed in the chaos. Was it not enough just to break through the guardian knights? Did I need a special item or some other condition?

I prepared to swing again out of instinct, until Yui popped out of my shirt pocket with a jingle. She touched the stone door of the gate with her tiny hand.

"Papa," she turned to me, speaking quickly, "this door isn't locked with a quest-related conditional! It's controlled by a system admin switch, nothing more."

"Wh-what does that mean?!"

"It means... nothing a player can do will open this door!"

"Wha..."

I was at a loss for words.

The grand quest at the center of the game—to reach the city atop the World Tree and be reborn as true fairies—was nothing more than a giant carrot, endlessly dangled out of reach of the game's player base? So not only was this battle's difficulty set to the extreme, the door was locked by nothing more than the will of the game manager...?

I felt my body go limp. The roars of the guardian knights bearing down washed over me, but I didn't even have the will to swing my sword anymore.

I was so close, Asuna, so close... I almost reached you... Will that little sliver of warmth you dropped to me be the last time we ever touch?

No, wait. Wasn't that...?

My eyes flew open. I stuck a hand in my waist pocket. Yes! The little card. Yui had called it a system access code...

"Yui, use this!"

I stuck the silver card in her face. Her eyes went wide and she nodded.

Yui brushed the card with one of her little hands. A few lines of light ran across the card and into her.

"I'm copying the code!" she shouted and slapped the surface of the gate with both hands.

I had to squint at the flash. Blue lines of light spread out from the spots Yui touched, and in moments, the entire gate glowed blindingly bright.

"It's copying! Grab hold, Papa!"

I touched her little hand with my fingertips. The lines of light passed through Yui and flowed into me.

Suddenly, I heard the scream of the guardian knights right behind me. I had barely even time to flinch before several of their massive swords bore down. But they passed right through me, as though the swords had no physical form. But in truth, it was I who was dematerializing. My body was fading away, blending with the light.

"—!!"

I felt a sudden tug pulling me forward. Yui and I became a flow of data, melting into the glowing white screen that had been the gate.

My mind was blank for only an instant.

I shook my head and blinked a few times, fighting off the after-effects of teleportation. This was similar to the symptoms of a teleport crystal back in Aincrad, but unlike the ever-present bustle of any city's teleport square, I had landed in the midst of absolute silence.

I slowly rose from a kneeling crouch. Yui greeted me, looking nervous. She was not a pixie anymore, but her original ten-year-old form.

"Are you all right, Papa?"

"Yeah. Where are we...?"

I looked around. It was a very...strange place. Unlike the

detailed and beautiful environs of Swilvane and Alne, which fit into the expectations of what a modern game looked like, this location was nothing but flat white surfaces with no details or textures whatsoever.

We seemed to be in the middle of a long hallway. It was not straight, but curved gently to the right. I looked behind me and saw a mirrored bend in the other direction. We were in a very long curve, or perhaps even a circle.

"I don't know. This place doesn't fall within the map info Nav Pixies have access to," Yui said, troubled.

"Can you tell where Asuna is?" I asked. She shut her eyes, and then almost instantly nodded.

"Yes, she's close—very close. Above us...this way."

She ran off silently, her bare legs flashing out of the familiar white dress. I put my greatsword over my back and hurried after her. The katana I'd been holding in my left hand was gone. When I teleported, it must have been automatically returned to Leafa, its proper owner. If she hadn't thrown it to me when she did, I would never have made it to the gate. I shut my eyes and said a silent word of thanks to the physical memory of its hilt in the palm of my hand.

After most of a minute running after Yui, a square door came into view on the left, the outer side of the curve. It, too, had no visual features whatsoever.

"We can go up from here."

I stopped next to Yui and took a glance at the side of the door—and froze.

There were two triangular buttons on the wall, one pointing up and one pointing down. I'd never seen their like in the game, but they were a familiar sight in the real world: elevator buttons.

I grimaced, suddenly feeling as though my battle armor and massive sword were completely out of place here. Except...it was this place that was strange. If these buttons meant what they appeared to signify, we were not within the game world. In that case, where were we?

That question left my mind as quickly as it formed. It didn't matter. Asuna was here.

I reached out and hit the upper arrow button without hesitation. The door *bing*ed and slid open, revealing a small, box-shaped chamber. Yui and I walked inside and turned around to find that there was indeed a panel of control buttons on the wall. Assuming the glowing one marked our current location, there were two floors above us. After a brief moment of indecision, I pushed the top button.

The chime sounded again and the door closed. I felt the unmistakable rising sensation of an elevator.

It stopped just as quickly. The door opened to reveal another curved hallway, identical to the one before. I turned to Yui, who was squeezing my hand.

"Is this the right level?"

"Yes. We're very close...She's just over there," Yui replied, pulling me onward.

We raced down the hallway for another minute, my heart beating faster and faster. Eventually we came to a door on the inner wall of the hallway, but Yui ran right past it without a glance. After a few more moments, she stopped at a nondescript point in the middle of the hall.

"...What is it?"

"There's a passage...through here," she murmured, rubbing the featureless outer wall. Her hand stopped still, and just as with the stone gate, blue lines of light began to run through the wall where she touched, wriggling away at right angles.

Thicker lines suddenly cut out a square piece of the wall, and with a brief buzz, it disappeared completely. Just as Yui had said, there was another plain white hallway extending out from the intersection.

The little girl headed down the new hallway silently, then sped up and broke into a run. Her young face was dark with desperation and haste. Asuna had to be near.

Faster, faster. It was the only thing on my mind as we raced down the corridor. Eventually it came to an end, a square door blocking our progress. Yui didn't bother to slow down, extending a hand to shove the door open.

"——!!"

We were greeted by a massive setting sun.

The world was surrounded by endless sunset. I had trouble processing what I was seeing at first, until I realized that I was standing at an unfathomably high altitude. The horizon was clearly curved from this vantage point. The wind howled in my ears.

I couldn't help but remember a similar moment, another view of infinite sunset as I sat side by side with Asuna, watching the end of Aincrad. Her voice echoed in my ears.

We'll always be together.

"Yeah—that's right. I'm back," I muttered, looking at my feet. It wasn't a platform of crystal, but a frightfully thick tree branch.

Finally my vision regained its proper sense of scale against the endless field of deep red. Overhead, leafy branches stretched out in all directions, as though supporting the very heavens above. Below were more and more branches, and past them was a thin layer of clouds. Far, far beyond that, I could see the faint reflection of a river surface as it wound through rolling fields.

I was on top of the World Tree. The peak of the world. The place that Leafa...that Suguha had dreamed of for so long.

But...

I slowly turned back. The giant wall that was the trunk of the tree stretched up and far away until it finally separated into more branches.

"There's no city in the sky..." I murmured. There was only those bland white corridors. They were not meant to be the city atop the tree, obviously. And if the setup for the main quest was correct, there would have been an in-game event after breaching the dome. But I didn't even get a musical fanfare, much less any explanation.

It was all an empty gift box. Past the enticing wrapping paper and ribbon, it was empty lies. How could I explain this to Leafa, after all of her dreams of being reborn as a high fairy?

"This is unforgivable…" I muttered at the unseen force or person overseeing this world. Something pulled at my right arm. Yui was looking up at me with concern.

"Oh, right. Let's go."

We could settle this once Asuna was safe. It was the only reason I was here, after all.

The large branch stretched ahead toward the sunset. An artificial path was carved into the center of the wood. What lay ahead was obscured by the growth of leaves, but through them I could see something gleaming and golden catching the light of the sun. We took off running toward it.

Several minutes of incendiary haste and desperation passed, driven by the thought that my long-awaited moment would arrive in just a matter of seconds. It seemed as though my sense of time was lengthening, each tick of the clock an eternity.

We pushed through the colorful, oddly shaped leaves and onward down the path. Little staircases went up and down each vertical undulation of the branch; I impatiently fluttered my wings and leaped them in a single bound.

Eventually the source of the golden light became clear. It was a grid of golden bars—no, a birdcage.

It was the classic round birdcage shape, tapering up to connect to a different branch overhead that ran parallel to ours. The only difference was its massive size. This was much too large to hold even a bird of prey, much less little songbirds. No, the cage was meant for something else.

I thought back to what Agil had said in his café, in a scene that felt like years ago at this point. Five players rode on each other's shoulders in an attempt to scale the World Tree, and they took a screenshot at the height of their flight. The picture showed a mysterious giant birdcage with a girl inside. *There's no doubt. Asuna—Asuna's in that thing.*

There was a strength and an urgency of certainty in Yui's tugging. We practically ran on the air, leaping down the final staircase. The branch grew much thinner as it approached the cage, coming to a tapered end where it reached the floor level. The interior of the golden birdcage was clearly visible now. The tiled floor was decorated with one large tree planter, along with a number of small pots with flowers of various types. In the center was a large canopy bed. To its side, a white table with a tall-backed chair. And seated on that chair, her hands folded and head lowered to the table in apparent prayer, was a girl.

Long, straight hair. A thin dress much like Yui's. Elegant, slender wings growing from her back. All shining red with the light of the sinking sun.

Her face was shrouded in shadows, but I knew who it was. I'd never mistake her. The magnetism of our souls was so strong it was practically visible, sparking with light in the space that separated us.

In that moment, that girl—Asuna—raised her head.

My deep, unending love had turned that familiar image into one beaming with sublime radiance. Her face was sometimes as finely beautiful as a sharpened blade, sometimes friendly with a mischievous warmth, but always at my side during the tragically short days we spent together. A look of shock ran through that familiar face, and her hands rose to her mouth. Her large hazel eyes rippled with a light that quickly turned into tears sitting upon her eyelashes.

I bounded forward the last several steps and whispered with a voice so weak it could not be heard.

"...Asuna."

At the same time, Yui cried, "Mama...Mama!!"

The very end of the branch intersected the cage, and there stood a door made of a tighter pattern of golden bars than the rest, complete with a small metal plate that appeared to be the lock. The door was closed, but Yui did not bother to slow down as she pulled me forward, swinging her right hand across her body. It was soon infused with a blue glow.

She swung her glowing hand back to the right, and the entire metal door and its plate blew off, vanishing in a flash of light.

Yui let go of my hand and threw her arms wide. "Mama!!"
She raced into the open cage.

Asuna leaped up so fast she knocked the chair backward. She had opened her arms as well, and the words came clearly from her trembling lips.

"Yui!!"

The little girl leaped and buried her face in Asuna's chest. Their long hair entwined, brown and black, glittering in the setting sun.

Yui and Asuna shared a fierce embrace, rubbing cheek to cheek, calling each other's name just to be certain it was truly the other.

"Mama…"

"Yui…Yui…"

The tears spilled from their eyes, sparkling like fire with the light of the sun before disappearing into the air.

I eased out of my run and walked over, stopping several steps away from Asuna. She raised her head, blinked a few tears away, and looked right at me.

Just like the other time, I couldn't move. If I approached any closer, reached out to touch her, she might vanish into thin air. And I didn't look anything like I did back then. My tanned sprig-gan skin and spiky hair were not at all like the old Kirito. All I could do was stare at her, trying to hold in my tears.

But just as she did before, Asuna spoke, calling my name.

"Kirito."

After a moment of silence, I called her name in return.

"…Asuna."

I took the last two steps forward, opening my arms and surrounding her fragile body, squeezing Yui between the two of us. My nostrils were full of her familiar scent, and my body was met with her familiar warmth.

"…I'm sorry it took so long," I moaned in a trembling voice, but Asuna just stared directly into my eyes.

"No, I knew you'd find me. I knew you'd come to save me…"

No other words were needed. Asuna and I closed our eyes and

each buried our face in the other's shoulder. Asuna's arms encircled my back and clung tight. Yui panted happily in between us.

It's all better now, I thought.

If this was to be my final moment, I would gladly burn away into nothing without a single regret. My life was meant to end with that world. I'd kept it going just so I could reach this instant and be complete...

No, that's not right. This is where it starts. Now the world of swords and battle is finally over, and we can start a journey together in a new world—reality.

I raised my head.

"C'mon. Let's go back to the real world."

After our embrace, Asuna and I still held hands, and Yui clung to Asuna's other arm. I looked down at her.

"Yui, can you manage to log Asuna out from here?"

She squinted and frowned for a moment, then shook her head.

"Mama's current status is tied down by some complicated code. I'll need a system console to undo it."

"A console," I repeated doubtfully.

Asuna's voice was tense. "I'm pretty sure I saw something like that on the bottom floor of the laboratory. Oh, the lab is the—"

"The white empty corridor?"

"Yes. You came here through there?"

"Yeah," I nodded. Asuna looked pensive.

"Were there any...weird things?"

"No, I didn't see anything on the way..."

"Well...there might be some of Sugou's henchmen lurking around. I just hope your sword will work on them!"

"Wait—Sugou?!" Shock, and then understanding, flooded through me. "This is...Sugou's doing? He locked you in here?"

"Yes, but that's not all. He's doing terrible things here..."

Asuna's face was dark with a deep rage, but she shook her head and stopped there.

"I'll tell you the rest when we get back to reality. Sugou's not at the office right now, as I understand it. We have to use this opportunity to crack the server and free everyone...Let's go."

I had plenty of questions to ask, but bringing Asuna back took priority over anything else. I nodded and spun around.

Asuna picked up Yui and I grabbed her hand, jogging back toward the blasted-out door frame. After a few steps I was stooping over to fit through the frame, and that was when it happened.

Someone was watching.

I felt a nasty tingling in the back of my neck. It was the exact same feeling I got in *SAO* when I was targeted, not by a monster but by another player with the orange cursor of a murderer.

Instantly, I let go of Asuna and put my hand on my sword. Just as I was pulling the hilt, the birdcage was doused in liquid. Then, with a deep-pitched splash, a dark, sticky substance completely covered us.

But that wasn't quite it; I could breathe, but the act was laborious. When I tried to move, there was an incredible pressure, like being stuck in a thick, viscous fluid. My body was crushingly heavy. It was agony just to stand.

At the same time, the color was draining from the world. The deep red of the sunset that had filled the cage was turning into blackness before my eyes.

"Wh-what is this?" Asuna shouted. Her voice was warped as though compressed by incredible water pressure.

Deeply disturbed by this phenomenon, I tried to spin around and hold Asuna and Yui safely at my side—but my body would not cooperate. The sheer adhesion of the air clung to me as though of its own malevolent will.

In time, the entire world was total darkness. But...that also wasn't entirely true. I could clearly see Asuna's and Yui's white dresses. It was as though every other surface of the world had been painted a perfect black.

I gritted my teeth and focused on moving my right hand. The

bars of the cage were right next to me. I tried to grab one and pull myself free of the immobilizing space, but my outstretched hand touched nothing at all.

It wasn't just an illusion. We had been plunged into an unknown world of darkness.

"Yui—"

I was going to ask her for an explanation, but she suddenly writhed in agony within Asuna's arms and screamed.

"*Aaah!* Papa, Mama...Be careful! Something...bad is—"

But before she could finish, purple light crawled across her small body. She flashed brightly—and then Asuna's arms were empty.

"Yui?!" Asuna and I screamed together. But there was no answer.

Only the two of us were left in the thick, sludgy blackness. I reached out desperately, trying to pull Asuna to my side. She did the same, her eyes wide with fear.

But before our fingertips could touch, we were assaulted by a tremendous gravity.

It was as though I'd been thrown into the bottom of a deep, deep swamp. I fell to a knee, unable to withstand the pressure. Asuna collapsed as well, both of her hands against the unseen floor.

She looked into my eyes and mumbled, "Kiri...to..."

I wanted to tell her that it was all right, that I would keep her safe no matter what. But before I could, a high-pitched, clinging voice echoed triumphantly through the darkness.

"And how are you enjoying my new spell? It's planned to go into the next update, but I'm wondering if it might not be a bit *too* strong?"

The voice was twisted with uncontrolled glee, but I recognized it. It was the voice that had ridiculed me as a "hero" before Asuna's comatose form.

"Sugou!" I growled, struggling to get back to my feet.

"Tsk, tsk! No using that name here, please. It is not fitting to speak to your king by name. You will address me as Your Majesty, King Oberon of the Fairies!"

His voice leaped even higher into a screech by the end, and something struck my head hard. I craned my neck to see a man standing right next to me. A leg in white tights ended in a gaudily embroidered boot that pushed against my head, rolling left and right.

Farther up, I saw a body covered by a toga in a venomous shade of green, and on top of that, a face so perfect it looked fake. But of course it was fake; it was a beautiful countenance created from scratch, so devoid of actual life that it was hideous. The crimson lips were twisted in a familiar gloating sneer.

Despite the different form, I would never mistake this man for anyone but Sugou. The man who'd been the target of all of my hatred, the one who'd stolen Asuna's soul and locked her in this place...

"Oberon—no, Sugou!" Asuna shouted. She was braced against the floor, only barely able to raise her head. "I've seen what you're doing here! The crimes you're committing... You won't get away with them, you can be sure of that!"

"Oh? And who's going to stop me? You? Him? God, perhaps? Sorry, sweetheart, there's only one God in this world: Me!"

He chuckled hideously and applied more pressure to my head. Unable to support the extra weight, I slumped to the floor.

"Stop it, you coward!!"

Sugou bent over, ignoring Asuna's insult, and pulled my sword from its scabbard. He held out the tip of his finger and set the blade spinning on it, perfectly vertical.

"I must say, Kirigaya—oh, pardon me, should I call you Kirito? I really didn't expect you to come all this way. I don't know if that makes you brave or an idiot. Given your current miserable predicament, I'd hazard to say it's the latter. Heh! I heard my little songbird had escaped her cage, so I rushed back to give her some much-needed discipline, only to find that—surprise! A cockroach had scuttled inside the cage! Along with some other strange little piece of code..."

Sugou trailed off and swiped his left hand to bring up the

menu. He stared at the blue screen with a frown on his lips for a bit, then snorted and closed the window.

"...It must have gotten away. What was that? How did you get up here, anyway?"

I was briefly relieved that Yui hadn't been deleted entirely, at least.

"I flew here. I've got wings."

"Hmph, whatever. I can just get the answer straight from your brain."

"...What?"

"You didn't think I created this entire scheme for kicks, did you?" Sugou bounced the sword lightly on the tip of his finger, leering venomously. "With the generous help of the former *SAO* players, my research into the basics of thought and memory manipulation is nearly eighty percent complete. In a very short time, I will achieve an unprecedented, godly feat: absolute control over the human soul! On top of that, I've got a brand-new test subject to play with. What fun! I can't wait to poke through your memories and rewrite your emotions! I'm getting chills just thinking about it!"

"You...can't do such a thing..."

His claims were so absurd that I could barely process them. Sugou put his foot back on my head and tapped his toe up and down.

"You didn't learn your lesson—you're plugged in with the Nerve-Gear again, aren't you? Which makes you no less helpless than any of my test subjects. Kids are so stupid. Even a dog knows it's made a mistake when it gets kicked."

"No...no, you can't do that, Sugou!" Asuna screamed, her face pale. "Don't you dare hurt him!"

"Little bird, the day is nigh that I can turn your hatred into subservience with the flip of a switch," Sugou replied, intoxicated with his own power. He grabbed my sword and pompously ran his fingers across the flat of the blade.

"But! Before I re-create your souls to my liking, let's have a little party! Finally…the moment I've been waiting for—the perfect guest has arrived. It truly was worth testing the very limits of my patience!"

He spun around and threw his hands wide. "I am now recording everything that happens within this space for posterity! Make sure you look good for the camera!"

"…"

Asuna bit her lip, looked me straight in the eye, and said, "Log out immediately, Kirito. You have to expose his conspiracy in the real world. I'll be fine."

"Asuna!"

For a moment, I was torn in two by indecision. But just as quickly, I agreed and waved my left hand. With this much information, I might be able to mobilize a rescue team, even without physical proof. If they could seize the *ALO* server within RCT Progress, everything would be clear.

But my window didn't appear.

"Ah-ha-ha-ha!" Sugou bent over with the force of his laughter. "I told you, this is my world! No one can escape it!!"

He walked around, hiccupping with laughter, and then suddenly raised his left hand. With the snap of his fingers, two jangling chains fell from the infinite blackness above.

A wide golden ring gleamed dully on the end of either chain. Sugou took one of them and snapped it around Asuna's wrist with a *click*. He gave a little tug on the chain, which extended up into the darkness.

"Aaah!"

The chain began to retract, and Asuna was hauled up by her right hand. It stopped at the exact point that the tips of her toes could barely touch the ground.

"What do you think you're doing?" I demanded, but Sugou ignored me and picked up the other ring, humming to himself.

"I've got plenty of props arranged for you. This will do for now, however," he said, snapping the other ring around Asuna's left wrist. The second chain rattled upward, and Asuna was left dangling in midair by her arms. The powerful gravity was still in effect, and her delicate eyebrows were twisted in pain.

Sugou crossed his arms in appreciation and whistled crudely.

"Nice. You don't get expressions like that with the NPC women."

"…!"

Asuna glared furiously at him, then shut her eyes against the pain. He chuckled and slowly walked around her back. He grabbed a handful of her long hair and then held it to his nose, breathing deeply.

"Mmm, that's a lovely scent. It was quite difficult to re-create the real Asuna's smell in-game—I had to hide an odor analyzer in her sickroom. Seems to me you ought to appreciate that kind of attention to detail."

"Stop it, Sugou!"

Uncontrollable anger surged through me. Red flames raced through my nerves, and for a moment, I was able to break the weight pinning me down.

"Gr…uh…"

I pushed myself off the ground with my right hand. Once I'd gotten up onto a knee, I concentrated all of my strength into trying to stand.

Sugou put a hand on his waist and shook his head theatrically. He walked over to me, mouth twisted.

"Good grief. The audience isn't supposed to be part of the show…Back to crawling!"

He kicked my legs out from under me, and I crumpled to the floor.

"*Gaah!*"

All the breath shot out of my lungs. I pushed up off the floor and raised my head to see Sugou, the corners of his mouth upturned in a poisonous grin, swinging my sword down upon me with all of his strength.

"*Gakh!*"

The sensation of the thick metal piercing my body sliced away the flames that had burned through all of my nerves. The blade exited my chest and wedged deep into the floor. There was no pain, but I was assaulted by an exceedingly rough and unpleasant sensation.

"K-Kirito!!" Asuna screamed. I looked to her, trying to tell her I was fine. But before I could speak, Sugou tilted his head back to the sky and crowed.

"System command! Set pain absorber to level eight!"

Suddenly I felt pain in my back—actual pain—like I'd been pierced with a sharp drill.

"Ngk...ahg..."

Sugou leered with delight at my obvious suffering. "Hch-heh. Oh, this is only the appetizer, my friend. I'll bump it up in stages as we go along. If I set the absorption level to three or lower, you'll remain in a state of shock even after logging out."

He clapped his hands with satisfaction and turned back to Asuna.

"L-let Kirito go right now, Sugou!" she cried, but he showed no signs of obeying.

"It's brats like him that I hate the most. No skills, no power behind him, but he sure knows how to run his mouth, the little maggot. Well, we know what happens to bugs—they get pinned into display cases. Besides, are you really in any position to worry about him, little bird?"

He extended a hand and traced Asuna's cheek from behind. She turned her head, trying to break free, but the powerful gravity kept her from moving.

His fingertips ran all over Asuna's face before sliding down her neck. Her features were twisted with disgust.

"Stop it...Sugou!" I shouted, trying desperately to push myself up again. Asuna managed a brave, trembling smile.

"It's all right, Kirito. I won't let this hurt me."

Sugou immediately cackled in his high-pitched voice. "That's what I like to hear. How long will you be able to maintain that pride—thirty seconds? An hour? An entire day? Do your best to prolong my pleasure, dear!"

As he spoke, he grabbed the red ribbon adorning the collar of Asuna's dress and ripped it right out of the cloth. The red fabric flew silently through the air like blood, landing in a limp heap next to me.

Pure white skin peeked out from the wide tear in the bodice of the dress. Asuna grimaced in shame, the corners of her tightly shut eyes twitching.

Sugou tilted his head in appreciation, smirking as he fondled her skin. His lips opened in a wide crescent, and a vivid red tongue snaked out. I could practically hear the sticky smacking as he licked her cheek.

"Heh-heh! Want to know what I'm thinking about right now?" he whispered madly into her ear, tongue still extended. "Once I've had my fun with you here, I'll visit your hospital room. I can lock the door, turn off the cameras, and it will be our little paradise, just you and me. I'll set up a nice big monitor, play the footage of today's recording, and enjoy it all over again with your real body. First I steal the purity of your heart—and then I ruin the chastity of your body! How fascinating! What a unique form of entertainment, don't you think?"

His falsetto cackling bubbled over, filled the darkness, and died out.

Asuna's eyes went wide for a moment, but she bravely knotted her lips. The unstoppable fear turned to two clear drops that lingered on her eyelashes. Sugou flicked out his tongue to taste them.

"Ahh...sweet, so sweet! Go on, give me more tears!"

Blinding white rage burned through my brain. All I could see were sparks.

"Sugou...*you son of a bitch*!!" I screamed, scrabbling wildly in an attempt to stand. But the sword running through me did not budge. I could sense tears forming in my own eyes now. I crawled like a miserable insect, writhing and bellowing.

"Damn you...I'll kill you! I swear it! You'll die by my hand!!"

But my screams were nearly drowned out by the sound of Sugou's mad laughter.

If you can just give me strength right now...

I prayed fervently, trying to move myself even a fraction of an inch forward, pulling against the ground with my fingertips.

If you can give me the strength to stand, I'll give up anything. My life, my soul, anything you want. I'll pledge it all to the devil or a demon if it helps me cut him down and return Asuna to where she belongs.

Sugou was running his hands over Asuna's arms and legs. Each move of his hand must have sent electronic signals of disgust to her sensory centers, because Asuna was biting her lip hard enough to draw blood as she withstood the defilement.

Though the image entered my eyes, all my brain saw was pure, burning white. The flames of anger and desperation consumed me. My neurons were turning into ash. Once I turned into a lump of dry, bone-white matter, I wouldn't think anything anymore. I wouldn't have to.

I thought I could do anything with a single sword at my side. I was the hero who stood at the pinnacle of ten thousand. The hero who defeated the evil sorcerer and saved the world.

It was a virtual world, just a game, developed by a business on basic marketing principles, and I'd imagined it was real. That the strength I found in the game was real strength. Had I been disappointed in the weakness of my actual body once I was released— exiled, more like it—from the world of *SAO*? Did a part of me wish that I could go back there, where I could be the greatest hero the world had ever known?

No wonder that when I'd learned that Asuna's mind was trapped in a new game world, I'd assumed that I could make it all better on my own, rather than letting those with true power, the adults of the real world, sort it out. I must have been very happy regaining my imaginary power, crushing other players and satisfying my ugly pride and self-esteem.

In that case, this was my just dessert. That's right—I was a child, playing with the power someone else had given me. I couldn't even overcome the simple ID system that granted a person system admin privileges. The only thing I was good at earning for myself was regret. If I couldn't handle that, my only escape was withdrawing from my mind altogether.

"You going to just run away?"

No, I'm only looking at reality.

"Giving in? To the power of the system you once denied?"

I can't help it. He's the game master, I'm only a player.

"You soil the memory of that duel with those words. You showed me that the human will could surpass a computer system. You helped me realize the future possibilities that our battle could bring about."

Battle? It's meaningless. A bunch of numbers going up and down.

"You know that's not true. Now get on your feet. Grab your sword."

"Stand up, Kirito!!"

It was like a bolt of lightning tearing through my wits, the voice the resulting clap of thunder. All of my wandering senses were connected in a single moment. My eyes shot open.

"Ugh…ah…" I couldn't produce anything but dry grunts. "Urh…rrgh…"

I gnashed my teeth and moaned like an animal close to death, but I did plant a hand on the ground and push myself onto an elbow. Attempting to lift my body only dug the heavy sword deeper into the small of my back.

I couldn't just lie there and crawl around miserably with this thing pinning me. I wouldn't let myself be crushed by such a soulless attack. Every one of the countless blades I'd suffered in *SAO* was heavier than this. More painful.

"Gr...raaah!!" I howled briefly, using every ounce of my strength and willpower to push myself up. The tip of the sword pulled out of the ground and finally fell out of my back, clattering beside me.

Sugou watched my unsteady rise to my feet with his mouth agape. He took his hands off of Asuna and glared at me, then shrugged theatrically.

"Oh, dear. I fixed that object's coordinates permanently, but it still came loose. Must be a few bugs left in the system. Those worthless, bungling programmers," he muttered, walking over and pulling his fist back to punch me.

My hand shot out and caught his in midair.

"Oh...?" He looked at me with suspicion again. I opened my mouth and spoke a string of commands that had lain dormant in my mind for months.

"System log-in. ID 'Heathcliff.' Password..."

After that came a complex assortment of letters and numbers. Once it was over, the crushing gravity pulling me down finally disappeared.

"Wh-what? What was that ID?!" Sugou yelped, teeth flashing. He snatched his fist away from me, leaping backward and swinging his left hand down to open the blue system window. But before his fingers could work the buttons, I entered another voice command.

"System command, adjust supervisor privileges. Set ID 'Oberon' to level one."

Sugou's window abruptly vanished. He looked back and forth from the empty space between his hands to my face several times, then swiped his hand again in irritation.

Nothing happened. The magic scroll that granted Sugou his fairy king powers had been spirited away.

"An...an ID with a higher clearance than mine...? That's impossible...It can't be...I'm the ruler, the creator...I am the emperor of this world...God..." he babbled, his voice so high-pitched it sounded like it was playing at double speed. His beautiful features were twisted and hideous.

"You know that's not true. You stole it. You stole this entire world and the people left in it. You're nothing but the king of thieves, dancing alone on the throne you stole from someone else."

"Why...you little brat...How dare you speak to me that way. You'll regret this insult...I'll tear off your head and hang it up as a decoration!"

He jabbed a twisted claw of a finger at me and screeched, "System command! Generate object ID 'Excalibur'!!"

But the system no longer heeded Sugou's voice.

"System command!! Obey me, you miserable heap of scrap! Your...your god commands you!!"

I tore my eyes away from the wailing Sugou to look at Asuna. The dress was nothing more than scraps loosely hanging on her body now. Her hair was tousled, and tear tracks gleamed on her cheeks. But those eyes had not lost their shine. Her hardy soul had not been broken.

I'll bring this to an end soon. Just give me a little time, I silently told her as I stared into her hazel-colored eyes. Asuna returned my signal with the slightest of nods.

The sight of Asuna's distress lit the fires of rage anew within me. I looked up and said, "System command. Generate object ID 'Excalibur.'"

The space in front of me. warped, tiny strings of numbers scrolling past to form a sword. Color and texture flowed upward through it from the tip. It was a beautifully detailed longsword, set with a dazzling gold blade. I recognized it as the sword sealed in the very bottom tip of the dungeon at the center of Jotunheim. There was something profoundly distasteful about producing the greatest sword in the game—the stuff of dreams to countless players—with a simple spoken command.

I grabbed the hilt of the sword and hurled it at the shocked Sugou. Once he had clumsily caught it, I brought my foot down hard on the pommel of my own sword; it clanged loudly and spun up into the air. I swiped my hand horizontally as the sword fell back to the earth, and caught it perfectly.

With the point of my massive dark blade pointed directly at Sugou, I issued my challenge.

"It's time to settle the score between the king of thieves and the so-called hero... System command, pain absorber to level zero."

"Wh... what...?"

That command had raised the sensation of virtual pain to an infinite amount. Panic flashed across the face of the fairy king, despite his golden sword. He faltered a step, then another.

"Don't chicken out. *He* never backed down from any situation—Akihiko Kayaba."

"K... Kaya..." He blanched when he heard that name. "Kayaba... Heathcliff. So it was you. You've come to ruin everything again!"

Sugou waved his sword in the air and screamed in a voice like tearing metal.

"You're dead! You kicked the bucket! How are you still interfering with my life after death? You always did this... always! Looking smug and serene, as if you understood everything... stealing everything I ever wanted from under my nose!"

He jabbed the point of his sword at me and continued. "You little cretin... what would you understand?! Do you have any idea what it was like to work under him, to compete and be compared to him at every turn?!"

"I do. I lost to him in a fight and had to be his servant—but I never wanted to be him. I'm not like you."

"You brat... you brat... you insolent little brat!!" he screeched, leaping at me with his sword drawn. Just as he came within range, I flicked my sword out. The tip grazed the fairy king's elegant cheek.

"Agh!" he yelped, holding his face and bouncing backward. "Aah... aaaah!"

The look of shock on his face only made me angrier. This man, this miserable *coward*, had kept Asuna prisoner for two months, tormenting her all the while? Intolerable.

I took a big step forward and swung straight down. Sugou put an arm up out of defensive reflex. The hand holding his golden sword was severed at the wrist and flew away into the darkness, landing with an audible *thump* somewhere far in the distance.

"*Aaaahh!!* My hand...my haaaand!!"

The pain he felt was false—only electronic signals—but as far as his brain knew, it was real agony. Yet, it was not enough to satisfy me. It couldn't possibly be enough.

Sugou bent over, clutching his maimed arm. I took a hearty swing at his green-clad torso.

"Gbwuah!!"

His tall body was cleanly sliced into two equal halves, and they fell heavily to the floor. His legs quickly burst into white flames and burned away.

I grabbed Sugou's flowing blond hair and lifted. Thick tears sprang from his wide, terrified eyes, and his mouth worked fiercely. There were no words coming out of it, only metallic screeching.

I felt nothing but disgust at the sight of him. With a toss of my hand, I flung his upper half straight up into the air and readied myself for a double-handed sword thrust. He reached the apex of the arc and came tumbling down, still bleating hideously.

"Haaah!!"

I swung with all of my strength. With a dull *chunk*, the sword struck through Sugou's right eye, and out the back of his head.

"*Eeyaaagh!!*"

His scream echoed unpleasantly through the darkness, like the screeching of a thousand rusty gears scraping into motion. Thick white flames erupted from his pierced eye, and soon licked across the rest of his head and torso.

Sugou did not stop screaming for the several seconds it took for him to be completely burned into nothing. His voice eventually faded out and vanished, and the world was silent again. I swiped my sword in satisfaction, scattering the little white flames that remained.

With an easy flick of my wrists, I severed the chains that had held Asuna prisoner. The sword's duty finished, I laid it on the floor and picked up her limp body.

It was at this point that the source of energy that had kept me going finally gave out as well. I slumped to my knees, and there gazed at Asuna in my arms.

"...Ngh..."

The feeling of miserable helplessness running through me leaked out of my eyes in the form of tears. I held her fragile body tight, burying my face in her hair, bawling. I couldn't speak. There were only tears.

"I always believed," Asuna's clear voice murmured next to my ear. "No...I still do believe. I did in the past, and I will in the future. You're my hero...You'll come to save me anywhere, anytime..."

Her hand brushed my hair.

No. That's not true. I don't have...any true strength...

I took a deep breath and managed to mumble, "I'll do my best...to make sure that's true. C'mon...let's go."

I waved my left hand and was greeted with a different, more complicated system window. I picked through it on instinct alone, digging through menu after menu for the teleportation-related commands.

With a deep stare into Asuna's eyes, I told her, "I think it's already nighttime in the real world. But I swear, I'll be at your hospital in no time."

"I know. I'll be waiting. I want you to be the first person I see with my real eyes."

She smiled, and with a distant gaze as calm as still water, she whispered, "So...it's finally coming to an end. I'm going back... to the real world."

"That's right...You'll be so surprised at everything that's changed."

"Hee-hee. You'll have to take me all over and show me a good time."

"Yeah. I will." I nodded and hugged her even harder. There was a targeted log-out button on the admin menu, and it turned my finger blue. I used that finger to trace the tracks of her tears, wiping them away.

Asuna's pale body in turn took on that vivid blue. Bit by bit, she grew transparent, delicate as a crystal. Little motes of light danced in the air, and she began to vanish, starting with the tips of her fingers and toes.

I held Asuna as tight as I could while part of her remained. Finally the weight left my arms, and I was alone in the darkness. I sat there, unmoving.

It felt like everything was over, yet it also felt like only a step in a larger process. This incident was the result of Kayaba's flight of fancy and Sugou's desire—but was this truly the end of it? Or was it only a part of some larger series of events?

I forced my aching, spent body to its feet and looked up, into the deep darkness over my head.

"I know you're there, Heathcliff."

After a brief silence, I heard the raspy voice echoing in my mind again, the way it had earlier.

"It has been quite a while, Kirito. Of course, to me, the events of that day might as well be yesterday."

Unlike just minutes ago, the voice seemed to be coming from some far-off place now.

"You're still alive?" I asked. The voice responded after a brief pause.

"You could say that, but you could also say the opposite. I am... an echo of Akihiko Kayaba's mind. An afterimage."

"Well, you make as little sense as he did. I guess I ought to thank you—though you could have helped a bit earlier than you did."

"..."

There seemed to be a tinge of chagrin in the silence.

"I apologize for that. It was only just recently that this program was reassembled and reactivated from its many hiding places within the system. Just at the moment that I heard your voice. Also, your thanks are unnecessary."

"...Why?"

"Too much has happened between us for altruistic favors. Every debt must be repaid."

Now it was my turn to grimace. "What do you want me to do?"

Out of the vast darkness fell something silver and shining. I reached out and caught the object. It was a small, egg-shaped crystal. A faint light flickered within it.

"What's this?"

"The seed of the world."

"What?"

"You will understand when it blooms. I leave its fate in your hands. Delete it, abandon it...but if you do happen to feel any emotion toward my world other than hatred..."

He let that statement hang. After a long silence, he said a brief farewell.

"I must be going. May we meet again, Kirito."

And just like that, he was gone.

I put the sparkling egg into my front pocket, confused. After a few moments, I had a sudden thought.

"Yui, are you there? You okay?"

Abruptly, the world of darkness shattered around me.

The orange light that had dyed the entire world before our confrontation ripped through the veil, bringing a breeze with it that blew away the blackness. I had to close my eyes against its radiance, and when I could open them without pain again, I was inside the birdcage.

Directly ahead, the sinking sun was releasing its final dying rays of light. I was alone, with only the sound of the wind for companionship.

"Yui?" I asked again. A light coalesced in the space before me, and a black-haired girl popped into existence.

"Papa!" she cried, throwing her arms around my neck.

"You're all right. Thank goodness…"

"Yes, my address was about to be locked, so I retreated into the NerveGear's local memory. When I connected again, you and Mama were both gone. I was so worried…Say, where is Mama?"

"She's back in the real world."

"I see…That's truly wonderful…"

Yui closed her eyes and laid her cheek against my chest, a shadow of sadness in her face. I gently caressed her long hair.

"She'll come back to see you very soon. But I wonder…what's going to happen to this world?" I murmured. Yui grinned.

"Well, my core program is in your NerveGear, not this realm. You can be with me forever. Oh, but there's something strange about all of this…"

"What is it?"

"There's a very large file being transferred to the NerveGear's local storage. It doesn't seem to be an active process, however…"

"Hmm," I said curiously, but I didn't bother to wonder about it for very long. There was more pressing business at hand.

"Well, I've got to go see Mama."

"Okay, Papa. I love you."

Yui squeezed me with all of her tiny strength, tears welling in her eyes. I rubbed her head and swiped my hand for the menu.

For a moment, I stopped to view the world as it lay shrouded in sunset. What would happen to it now, this world with its false king? The thought of Leafa and the other players who cared so deeply for Alfheim made my heart hurt.

I gave Yui a gentle kiss on the cheek and tapped a few commands. Light burst out from the point ahead of me, swallowed my consciousness, and pulled me higher, higher.

When I opened my deeply exhausted eyelids, the first thing I saw was Suguha's face. She was watching me with a fretful expression, but when our eyes met, she bolted upright.

"S-sorry for sneaking into your room. I got worried when you never returned," she said, sitting on the edge of the bed with a trace of red in her cheeks. After a brief time lag for recovery, I tensed my limbs to return the strength to them after my long play session, then bounced up to a sitting position.

"Sorry for taking so long."

"Is it...all over?"

"Yeah. It's over...It's all over," I murmured, staring into nothing. I couldn't possibly tell Suguha that I'd nearly been taken prisoner again, and this time in a prison without a victory condition to free me. The time would eventually come to explain it all to her, but I didn't want to cause her any unnecessary concern for now. This sister of mine, my only sibling, had already saved me in more ways than I had words to express.

My new adventure began in that deep forest that night, when I happened across the girl with green hair—and she'd been at my side for the entire long journey. She'd shown me the way, explained the world's customs, and swung her sword to protect me. Thanks to her guidance, I'd met two leaders within the game, without whose help I would never have broken through the wall of guardian knights.

I realized upon reflection that I'd been helped by a great many people. But first and foremost, by the girl in front of me now. Leafa had helped Kirito, and Suguha, Kazuto; and during the entire time, she'd been grappling with her own deep, troubling feelings.

It was a good moment to take a new look at Suguha's face, a combination of bright, masculine vitality and the fragility of a freshly budded flower shoot. I reached out and caressed her cheek, and she smiled shyly.

"Thanks for everything, Sugu—I mean it. I couldn't have done any of it without you."

She looked down, face beet-red, and fidgeted. Eventually she made up her mind and leaned her cheek against my chest.

"It's okay...I was happy to do it. Happy to be helpful to you in your world," she said, eyes closed. I slipped my arm around her back and gave her a gentle squeeze.

Once I'd let go, she looked up and said, "So...you got her back? Asuna, I mean..."

"Yeah. She's back—finally back. Sugu...I..."

"I know. Go see her. I'm sure she's waiting for you."

"I'm sorry. I'll explain everything when I get back."

I patted the top of Suguha's head and got to my feet.

In record time, I was pulling on my down jacket in the yard, ready for the trip. It was night outside. The old standing clock in the living room said it was just before nine—well after visiting hours, but if I explained the circumstances at the nurse's desk, they would surely let me in.

Suguha trotted over and offered me a nice, thick sandwich. I gratefully stuffed it into my mouth and descended into the yard.

"Brr, it's cold..."

I hunched my shoulders. The chill seemed to pass right through my jacket. Suguha looked up at the night sky and said, "Oh... snow."

"Huh...?"

There were indeed two or three large snowflakes glittering through the air. For a moment, I considered using a taxi, but decided that racing on my bike was a quicker trip than walking out to the main road and trying to find a cab.

"Be careful...Say hi to Asuna for me."

"I will. I'll give you a proper introduction next time."

I waved good-bye to Suguha, hopped onto my mountain bike, and started pedaling.

The trip across the southern part of Saitama Prefecture went by incredibly fast with my single-minded bicycle sprint. The pace of the snow picked up, but not enough to pile up on the side of the road, and, thankfully, that kept the amount of traffic on the streets low.

I wanted nothing more than to be in Asuna's hospital room as soon as possible—but there was a part of me that feared it as well. I'd spent every other day for two months visiting that place and knowing only deep, deep disappointment. I would take my sleeping princess's hand, so still I was afraid she'd turned into a sculpture of ice, and call out to her, knowing full well she would not hear.

As I raced down streets so familiar that I knew where all the potholes were, I couldn't shake a part of me that wondered if my discovery of her in the land of the fairies, the vanquishing of the false king, and the severing of her chains…were all nothing more than hallucinations.

What if, several minutes from now, I visited her room to find that she was not awake?

What if her soul had already left Alfheim and gone not to the real world, but to some other, unknown place?

A terrifying chill ran down my back that had nothing to do with the snow pelting my face in the darkness. It couldn't happen. The system that ran the game of real life would not be designed so cruelly.

My thoughts writhed and tangled, but I kept pedaling. After a right on the main route, I headed into the hills. The deep, block-pattern treads of my tires chewed the asphalt and its light layer of sherbet snow. I kicked the pedals into a higher gear.

Eventually the shape of a large, dark building came into view. Most of the windows were black, and the blue guiding lights around the helicopter landing pad on the roof blinked like ghostly wisps floating around a castle of darkness.

At the top of the final hill was a tall fence. I rode along the perimeter for another minute until the front entrance came into view, flanked by tall gateposts.

Because this was a special cutting-edge hospital that did not take emergency patients, the gate was shut tight and the guard box was unattended. I passed the main entrance en route to the parking area, where a small employee gate to the grounds had been left open.

I left my bike in the corner of the parking lot, too impatient to bother locking it up. The parking lot was completely empty, lit only by the orange sodium-vapor streetlights. The only thing moving was the silent snow, painting the world white around me as it fell. I ran, my heavy breathing creating dense clouds of vapor.

When I was halfway across the vast parking lot, I was about to pass between a tall, dark van and a white sedan when a silhouette emerged from behind the van and nearly collided into me.

"Ah…"

I was about to apologize as I avoided the figure—until the menacing gleam of something sharp and metallic swiped out at me.

"——?!"

A sharp burning sensation burst across my right forearm just below the elbow, and a great number of white things spilled into the air. Not snow—fine, tiny feathers. The lining of my down jacket.

I stumbled backward, only managing to stay upright by leaning against the rear of the white sedan.

I stared, stunned, at the black silhouette standing six feet away. It was a man. A man wearing a dark suit. There was something long and white in his right hand. It glowed in the dull orange light.

A knife. A large survival knife. But why?

I could sense the man, standing in the shadows cast by the tall van, examining my freezing face. He spoke, his voice ragged and quiet as a whisper.

"You took so long, Kirito. What if I'd caught a cold?"

That voice. That high-pitched, wheedling voice.

"S…Sugou…" I murmured in a daze. He took a step forward, and the orange light of the streetlamps hit his face.

The hair that had been so neatly styled at our meeting several days ago was wild and bedraggled. There was a shadow of a beard on his pointed chin, and his necktie hung loose around his neck.

But most of all, I noticed the bizarre look in his eyes through the metal-framed glasses he wore. Almost immediately, I realized what was so strange about it. His narrow eyes were bulging wide, the pupil of his left eye dilated and trembling in the low light—but his right pupil was constricted tight. The exact same spot that I'd pierced in our fight atop the World Tree.

"That was so very cruel of you, Kirito," he growled. "The pain won't go away. Not that I'm worried—I've got plenty of drugs for that."

Sugou reached into his pocket and removed a few pills that he promptly tossed into his mouth. He crunched them heartily and took another step forward. By now I'd finally recovered from the shock, and managed to speak through dry lips.

"You're finished, Sugou. You can't hide something that huge. Give up and face justice."

"Finished? How so? Nothing is finished. True, RCT may be useless now. But I'm going to America. There are plenty of companies who want me over there. I've got plenty of data from my experiments. If I can use them to complete what I started, I can be a true king—a god—the god of the *real* world."

He's gone mad. No...this man had probably broken long before.

"I just have a few things to clean up first. For starters, I'm going to kill you, Kirito," Sugou muttered, expression locked in place. Then he lunged toward me, stiffly jabbing his knife at my stomach.

"...!!"

I barely evaded. An attempt to leap off the asphalt with my right foot was aborted when snow stuck in the sole of my shoe caused me to slip and crash to the pavement. I landed hard on my left side, the breath shooting from my lungs.

Sugou gazed down at me with his mismatched eyes.

"Get on your feet."

The tip of his expensive leather shoe stomped into my femur once, twice, and again. Hot pain shot through my spinal cord deep into my brain. The impact rattled my wounded arm, which throbbed painfully. It was only then that I realized he'd actually cut my arm, not just the sleeve of my jacket.

I couldn't move. I couldn't speak. The terrible murderous pressure of Sugou's survival knife—a good eight inches long—froze the blood in my veins.

Kill... me... that knife—?

Only fragments of thoughts could find purchase in my scrambled wits. All my circuits were busy imagining, over and over, that fateful moment when the thick knife silently invaded my body, delivering the fatal blow. It was the only thing I could do.

The throbbing in my right arm turned to a burning numbness. Black liquid was dripping from between my jacket sleeve and winter gloves. I imagined all the blood in my body flowing out of me. Death—not based on numerical hit points, but true, actual death.

"C'mon, stand. Get up." Sugou kicked my legs repeatedly, mechanically. "What was it you were saying to me back there? About not running? Not being a coward? Settling our score? How brave and bold you were."

His whispering was laced with the same madness I'd heard in the midst of that suffocating darkness.

"Don't you understand? Little boys like you who only know how to play video games have no real power. You're scum, the garbage of society. And yet you had the audacity, the temerity to ruin my plan... There can be no punishment but death. Death is the only solution," he droned.

Sugou rested his foot on my stomach and shifted his weight forward. That physical force, combined with the mental pressure of his madness, took my breath away.

I could do nothing but watch his approaching face and gasp in short, irregular bursts. Sugou craned over and raised his weapon high.

Without a blink, he swung it down.

"——!"

The only sounds were a muted grunt from the back of my throat and the dull *crunch* of the knifepoint grazing my cheek and digging into the asphalt beneath me.

"Oopsie...Hard to aim when only one eye works," he muttered, and pulled his hand back for another try.

The knife's edge, catching the glow of the parking lot lights, was an orange line against the darkness. The very tip was chipped from its direct impact against the hard pavement. That flaw, the ugly imperfection of it, gave the knife a greater sense of physical realism. It was not a weapon made of perfect polygons, but a compact mass of metal molecules: sharp, cold, heavy, deadly.

Everything moved slowly. The snowflakes falling through the dark sky. The foggy breath from Sugou's curved mouth. The edge of the knife as it descended toward me. The gleaming orange reflection of the blade, flickering with the serrated pattern on its back.

I remember a weapon that was jagged like that, my brain subconsciously muttered to itself, piecing together fragments of meaningless memory.

What was it again? A dagger-type item sold in the one of the cities around the middle of Aincrad. It was called a swordbreaker. The back was serrated like a saw to parry the enemy's blow, with a small bonus chance to break their weapon. I was intrigued enough to put my Dagger skill in an empty slot and try it out, but I was never satisfied with its meager attack power.

The weapon in Sugou's hand now was smaller than that, not even large enough to be called a dagger. In fact, this would hardly be labeled a weapon—it was an everyday tool. It was not a weapon that a swordsman would use in a fight.

Sugou's words of a few seconds ago echoed in my ears.

You have no real power.

He was right, of course. There was no need to point it out. *But what does that make you in your attempt to kill me, Sugou? A master knife wielder? Do you know how to fight?*

I stared at the bloodshot eyes behind Sugou's glasses. Agitation. Madness. But there was something else as well: It was the look of a man trying to escape. They were the eyes of wild instinct, of he who lashes out with abandon with his back to the wall, trapped by monsters deep inside a dungeon with little hope for escape.

He was just like me, struggling miserably in search of power that he never found.

"Die, boy!!"

Sugou's scream snapped me from the decelerated world of thought back to the present. My left hand shot up and caught Sugou's wrist in descent, while I reached out and jammed the base of his throat with my other thumb, just above his necktie.

"*Hurgk!*" he yelped, lurching backward. I lunged and grabbed his wrist with both hands, scraping the backside against the frozen asphalt. He screeched and relaxed his grip. The knife clattered to the ground.

Sugou lunged for the blade, screaming wheezily like some kind of whistle. I pulled back my right leg and planted a stomp with the sole of my shoe against his chin. From there, I scooped up the knife and got to my feet.

"Sugou," I growled, my voice foreign and guttural. The knife's presence was hard and cold through my glove. It was a weak weapon. Too light, too short.

"But it'll be enough to kill you," I muttered, and leaped onto Sugou, who was sitting on the asphalt stunned, mouth agape.

I grabbed a fistful of hair with my left hand and slammed his head against the van door. The aluminum body dented inward and his glasses went flying. Sugou's mouth was wide in a gasp of shock. I pulled the knife back, preparing to jab it at his exposed throat.

"Grrh...aaah!"

But I had to stop, to grit my teeth against the urge.

"Hyeeek!! Eeyaaa!!"

Sugou was emitting the exact same high-pitched squeals that I'd heard in Alfheim not even an hour ago. He deserved to die. He deserved to be judged. If I brought the knife down now, everything would be over at last. Finished. The decisive separation of winner and loser.

But...

I was not a swordsman anymore. The world where skill with the sword decided everything was a relic of the distant past now.

"Eeeeh..."

Sugou's eyes suddenly rolled back into his head. His scream ended abruptly, and he slumped to the ground like a robot unplugged.

The tension drained out of my arm. The knife slipped through my fingers and landed on Sugou's midsection. I let go of him and got to my feet.

If I spent another second looking at this hateful man, the urge to kill would return, and I would not be successful at stifling it twice.

I pulled off Sugou's necktie, laid him out on the ground, and tied his hands together behind his back. The knife went onto the roof of the van. Then I turned away and forced my stumbling body to make its way, step by clumsy step, across the parking lot.

It took five minutes to climb the wide steps to the front entrance. I stopped there, breathing heavily, and took a look down at my body.

I was a mess, filthy with snow and grit. My right arm and left cheek were throbbing painfully, but the bleeding had stopped, at least.

The front door was automatic, but it showed no sign of opening. I peered through the glass to see that the lights of the lobby were dim, but it was brighter back at the reception counter. Fortunately, there was an unlocked glass push door on the left side that offered me a way in.

The interior of the building was silent. I walked past rows of benches lining the spacious lobby. The counter was unattended, but I could hear laughing coming from the nurse station behind it. I prayed that I could make my voice heard.

"Um...excuse me!"

After a few seconds, the door opened and two women in pale green uniforms appeared. They looked pensive at first, but that turned to shock when they got a better look at me.

"What happened?!" said one of them, a tall, young nurse with her hair tied up. My cheek must have bled more than I realized.

I pointed back to the entrance and said, "A man with a knife attacked me in the parking lot. He's knocked out next to a big van."

They looked nervous. The older nurse went over to a device behind the counter and leaned into a microphone.

"Security, please come to the first-floor nurse station at once."

The patrolman must have been close, because within seconds a man in a navy-blue uniform came trotting over. When the nurses repeated my description, his face went hard. He said something into a small comm unit and headed for the entrance. The younger nurse went with him.

The other nurse took an appraising look at the cut on my cheek.

"You're the family of Ms. Yuuki up on the twelfth floor, aren't you? Is that your only injury?"

She seemed to be under a slight misconception, but I nodded anyway. I didn't have the willpower to correct her.

"I see. I'll call the doctor at once. Just wait here." She hurried off.

I took a deep breath and looked around the lobby. Once I was sure there was no one around, I slipped behind the counter and grabbed a guest pass. With my access in hand, I set my trembling legs working in the direction that none of the adults had gone— toward the hallway I'd traveled dozens of times before.

The elevator was parked on the first floor, so the door opened as soon as I hit the button. I leaned against the interior wall as the car headed for the top floor. As it was a hospital elevator, its progress was gentle, but even that slight increase in pressure felt ready to break my knees. I barely stayed upright.

After endless seconds, the elevator stopped and the doors opened. I practically crawled into the hallway.

The few yards to Asuna's room felt like miles. I had to prop myself against the handrail along the wall just to keep moving. Left at the L-shaped turn in the hallway, and there was the white door, straight ahead.

Step after step after step.

Back then, too—

After the virtual world's sunset-wrapped demise, I was released to reality. I woke up in a nondescript hospital room, and that day I made a journey on stumbling feet. In search of Asuna, I walked and walked. That path had led me to this moment.

Finally, I would meet her. The time had come.

As the distance grew shorter, the emotion grew hotter and more fervent within me. My pulse raced. My vision began to fade. But I couldn't pass out here. So I walked. Step after step after step.

I was so intent on that process that I nearly walked right into the door before I realized where I was.

Asuna was on the other side. That was my only thought.

I reached out a trembling hand, but the keycard slipped through my sweaty fingers, onto the floor. I picked it up and tried again, successfully sticking it into the slot on the metal plate. Breath held, I slid it back out.

The light on the plate changed color, a motor whirred, and the door opened.

The scent of flowers drifted outward.

There were no lights on inside, only the faint white glow of the outside illumination reflecting off the snow.

As usual, the room was split through the middle by a large curtain. The gel bed was on the other side.

I couldn't move. I couldn't continue. I couldn't speak.

A sudden whisper sounded in my ear.

"Go on—she's waiting."

I felt a hand push my shoulder. Yui? Suguha? Someone's voice had saved me in three different worlds. I picked up my right foot and brought it down. Then my left. Then my right again.

The curtain was right ahead. I reached out and grabbed it.

Pulled.

The white veil rolled aside with a sound as gentle as the breeze over a field.

"...Ahh," the sound escaped from my throat.

A girl, wearing a thin white hospital gown that looked almost like a dress, was sitting upright. She faced the dark window, her back to me, and the quiet glow from the falling snow shone in her long, lustrous hair. Her thin arms were resting in her lap, holding a shining, blue, egg-shaped object.

Her NerveGear. The crown of thorns that had held her prisoner for so long was finally silent, its job finished.

"Asuna," I said, my voice a whisper. She jumped, stirring the flower-scented air, and turned.

The hazel eyes that looked at me were still full of the dreamy light of one awakened from a long, long sleep.

How many times had I imagined this moment? How many times had I prayed for it?

A smile floated to her pale, graceful lips.

"Kirito."

It was the first time I had heard that voice. It was quite unlike the one I'd heard every day in Aincrad. But this voice, actual vibrations in the air that hit my actual eardrums en route to my brain, was many times more wonderful.

Asuna took her left hand off the NerveGear and reached out. It was trembling slightly—even this act was exhausting to her.

I took her hand as gently as I could, as though holding a sculpture of snow. It was painfully thin and frail—but warm. The warmth of our contact seeped into us, as though to heal all wounds. All the strength went out of my legs, and I had to lean against the edge of the bed.

She brought her other hand up to touch my wounded cheek, tilting her head in question.

"Yeah...the final—the *true* final—battle just finished. It's over..."

And at last, tears sprang to my eyes. The wetness dripped down my cheeks, onto her fingers, shining with the light from the window.

"I'm sorry...I can't really hear yet. But...I know what you're saying," she whispered, rubbing my cheek with care. Just the sound of her voice shook my soul.

"It's over...It's finally over...I've finally met you."

Shining silver tears streamed down Asuna's cheeks as well and dripped off her chin. Her wet eyes stared deeply into mine, as though attempting to tell me everything within her mind.

"It's nice to meet you. I'm Asuna Yuuki. I'm back, Kirito."

I held in a sob and responded, "I'm Kazuto Kirigaya. Welcome home, Asuna."

We leaned forward and brushed lips, lightly. Then again, harder.

I put my arms around her fragile body and held her gently.

The soul travels. From world to world. From this life to the next.

And it seeks others. Calls out.

Long ago, in a big castle floating in the clouds, a boy who dreamed of being a warrior and a girl who loved to cook met and fell in love. Those two are gone, but after a long, long journey, their hearts met again.

I gently rubbed Asuna's back as she sobbed, watching out the window with tear-blurred eyes. Beyond the falling snow, which was coming down harder than before, I thought I saw two silhouettes standing together.

A boy in a black coat, with two swords crossed over his back.

A girl in a knight's uniform, red on white, with a silver rapier at her waist.

They smiled, held hands, and walked off into the distance.

9

"That's all for today's class. I'll be sending you files twenty-five and twenty-six for homework, so make sure you complete and upload them by next week."

An electronic chime mimicking the sound of a bell signaled the end of the morning classes. The teacher turned off the wide-screen monitor, and the mood in the classroom relaxed.

I used the old-fashioned mouse plugged into my computer unit to open and view the downloaded homework files. The wall of text that popped up made me sigh. I unplugged the mouse, flipped the screen closed, and tossed them both into my pack.

The sound of that chime was dangerously close to the bells of the chapel in the Town of Beginnings on the first floor of Aincrad. If that was by design, whoever had put together this school had a sick sense of humor.

None of the students in their matching uniforms seemed to notice or care, though. They chattered happily, leaving the class-room in small groups and heading for the cafeteria.

I closed the zipper on my backpack and was slipping it over my shoulder when the boy who sat next to me looked up and said, "Going to the cafeteria, Kazu? Save me a seat, yeah?"

Before I could respond, the student on the other side of him grinned and piped up, "Nah, man. Today's Kazu's audience with the princess."

"Oh, right. Lucky sap."

"Yep, that's right. Sorry, guys."

I waved a brief good-bye and left the classroom before their usual complaints could pick up steam.

Only once I'd hurried down the light green hallway and out the emergency exit into the courtyard could I breathe a sigh of relief away from the bustle of the lunch hour. A fresh new brick path started at the door and wound through lines of sapling trees. The plain concrete building that loomed over the branches was nothing special to look at, but for a school thrown together using an old building left unused after school district consolidation, it was an impressive campus.

After I spent a few minutes walking through the tunnel of greenery, the brick path led me to a small, circular garden. The outer perimeter was decorated with a number of flower beds and plain wooden benches. Sitting on one of them was a female student, looking up at the sky.

Her long brown hair fell straight down the back of her deep green school blazer. Her skin was a pale white, but a rosy blush had recently returned to her cheeks.

Her slender legs were extended forward, held neatly together, and covered in long black socks. Her brown loafers were tapping in rhythm on the bricks as she stared into the azure sky. The sight was so endearing that I had to stop at the entrance of the garden, hang on a tree branch, and watch.

When she looked down and noticed me, her face cracked into a smile. Then she closed her eyes and turned her face away in a satisfied pout.

I grimaced and approached the bench.

"Sorry to keep you waiting, Asuna."

Asuna glanced at me and frowned. "Why do you always have to watch me from the shadows?"

"Sorry, sorry. Maybe it turns out I have some stalkerish qualities after all."

"Ugh..." She drew back, looking disgusted, as I plopped down next to her and yawned.

"Man...I'm so tired...and hungry..."

"You sound like an old man, Kirito."

"Well, I sure feel like I aged five years in the past month. Plus"—I folded my hands behind my head and shot her a sidelong glance—"it's Kazuto, not Kirito. It's against proper etiquette to use character names here."

"Oh, right. I always forget...Hey, what about me? Everyone knows mine now!"

"That's what you get for using your own name for a handle. Not that mine is that well hidden..."

All the students at this special school were former players of *Sword Art Online* who had been in middle or high school at the time of the incident. The actual orange players who had actively engaged in murder within the game were forced to submit to at least a year of counseling and monitoring for the sake of their mental health, but there were many players—including me—who'd been forced to attack others out of self-defense, and there was no official record or means of determining who had engaged in crimes like theft or extortion.

So it was considered taboo to mention one's name within Aincrad, in order to avoid the settling of old scores. On the other hand, our faces were the same as they'd been in *SAO*. Asuna was discovered as soon as she stepped into the school building, and among some of the old high-level players, my nickname was common knowledge.

Naturally, it was impossible to expect that everything could be swept under the rug as though it never happened. The things that happened over there were real, not a dream, and every person here would have to find their own way to come to terms with those memories.

Asuna was holding a woven basket in her lap. I reached over and took her left hand in both of mine. It was still too thin, but it had filled out quite a lot since the day she'd awakened.

Her physical rehab had been quite fierce in order for her to make the start of the school term. She'd only recently been able to walk without crutches again, and she was still forbidden from any exercise, including running.

I visited her in the hospital after her awakening just as often as before, and it had been agonizing to watch her struggle to walk with the supports, teeth gritted and tears in her eyes. I rubbed her slender fingers over and over, remembering how hard it had been.

"...Kirito."

I looked up. There was color in Asuna's cheeks.

"Are you aware the cafeteria looks directly down onto this garden?"

"Wha...?"

Sure enough, on the top floor of the building over the tops of the trees were the tinted windows of the cafeteria. I let go abruptly.

"Honestly," she sighed, then turned away in a huff again. "Forgetful people don't get to have their lunches."

"Aaah, I'm sorry!"

I apologized profusely for several seconds, until Asuna finally smiled and opened the basket sitting in her lap. She pulled out a round object wrapped in kitchen paper and handed it to me.

I hurriedly opened the paper to find a large hamburger with lettuce jutting out from the sides. The scent hit me directly in the stomach, and I jammed it into my mouth.

"Mm...diffwavor..."

I chewed ravenously, swallowed to clear my throat, and then gave Asuna a wide-eyed look of surprise. She smiled and said, "Heh-heh. You remember it?"

"How could I forget? It's the hamburger we ate at the safe haven on the seventy-fourth floor..."

"It was really hard to re-create the exact flavor, actually. It's just not fair, you know? I worked myself to death trying to copy a realistic taste back there, and now I'm working myself to death trying to re-create it again back here."

"Asuna..."

I stared at her, a storm of emotions raging in my chest at all of those happy memories. She looked right back at me and grinned.

"You have mayo on your cheek."

By the time I'd finished my two large sandwiches and Asuna had eaten her small one, the lunch period was nearly over. She was holding a paper cup full of steaming herb tea from her thermos when she asked, "What's on your schedule after lunch?"

"I've got two more classes, I think. It's so weird. We've got EL panels rather than blackboards, tablets rather than notebooks, and our homework gets sent through wireless LAN—at this rate, we might as well just take our classes from home," I grumbled. Asuna giggled.

"The screens and PCs might only be temporary. Pretty soon everything will be holographic...Besides, coming to school means we can actually meet up like this."

"Good point..."

We made sure to share all of our electives, but since we were in different years, our main curriculum kept us apart. We only actually saw each other in class three days a week.

"Plus, Father says this is a model case for the next generation of schools."

"Ahh...How is Shouzou?"

"Well, he was pretty bummed for a while. Said he was no judge of character after all. He's been half-retired since leaving the CEO position, so I think he's looking for a good way to deal with the lack of pressure on his shoulders. He'll be fine once he finds a hobby."

"I see..."

I took a sip of tea and joined Asuna in gazing up at the sky.

Asuna's father, Shouzou Yuuki, had long ago decided on Asuna's future husband—Nobuyuki Sugou.

After he was arrested in the hospital parking lot on that snowy night, Sugou continued to struggle and wriggle to avoid what he deserved. He kept his silence, he denied all wrongdoing, and he ultimately tried to pin everything on Akihiko Kayaba.

But once one of his subordinates was called in for questioning, everything came out into the open. He revealed that the three hundred victims of *SAO* who had not returned were held captive within a server in the Yokohama office of RCT Progress, victims of inhumane mind control experiments. Sugou was truly done for, but he did appeal for a psychiatric examination when the trial started. His primary charges were based on assault, but the public was curious to see if they could tag him with abduction.

It soon became clear that his shocking experiment on full-dive brainwashing was only possible through the first-generation NerveGear unit. They had all supposedly been destroyed, and with the results of Sugou's experiment, it would be possible to design protection to ensure it could never happen again.

There was at least one piece of good news: None of the newly released survivors had any memory of the experiment. They suffered no physical tissue damage nor any psychological scars, so with the benefit of proper recuperation and counseling, all three hundred would be able to reassimilate into society.

But RCT Progress and *ALfheim Online*, if not the VRMMO genre as a whole, suffered a fatal blow.

Society was already wary enough after the *SAO* incident. So when *ALO* came along, the implicit promise to consumers was that the incident had been the work of a lone madman, and the VRMMO concept itself was still safe. But after Sugou's handiwork, the public opinion was that any VR game could be used to commit a heinous crime.

Ultimately, RCT Progress was disbanded and RCT itself suffered heavy losses, but with a changing of the guard in senior management, the company was attempting a recovery.

ALO was shut down, of course, and five or six other VRMMOs in service, though losing only a slight number of members, were taking massive heat from the public sphere. Most speculated that they would all eventually be canceled as well.

It was only through a surprise twist of fate that this state of events was overturned...

...by the "seed of the world" Akihiko Kayaba left to me.

The issue of Kayaba must be addressed.

It was two months ago, in March 2025, that the suspicions were confirmed: Akihiko Kayaba had indeed died with the collapse of *SAO* in November 2024.

For the two years that he ruled over Aincrad as Heathcliff, Kayaba had been staying in a secluded mountain cabin deep in the woods of Nagano Prefecture.

Of course, his personal NerveGear had no deadly shackles built into it, and he was able to log out whenever he wanted, but there were records of continuous log-in time of up to a week as he carried out his guild leadership duties.

Assisting him during those times was a fellow researcher and graduate student at the industrial college he'd been affiliated with, even as he worked at Argus.

Both she and Sugou had been students at Kayaba's lab, and by all outward appearances, Sugou had both respected Kayaba and felt a powerful rivalry toward him. Sugou had pursued the assistant romantically as well, a fact I learned from her after she was released on bail last month.

I forced the agent from the emergency response team to cough up her e-mail address and, after much careful consideration, sent her a message claiming that I didn't want to blame her for anything, I only wanted to ask some questions. Her response came a week later. The woman's name was Rinko Koujiro, and she traveled to the city from her home in Miyagi, to meet me at a café near Tokyo Station.

Kayaba had decided, even before he put his plan into motion, that he would die when the world of *SAO* collapsed. However, his choice of method was quite bizarre. He used a modified full-dive

machine to perform a high-powered scan of his entire brain, fry-
ing it in the process.

The odds of the scan working successfully were only one in
a thousand, she claimed. I found her to be both fragile and yet
inwardly tough at the same time.

If all went according to his plan, he would be copying his memories and thoughts in the form of digital code so that he could
exist within the network as an electronic brain.

I grappled with this information a bit, but eventually told her
that I'd spoken with Kayaba's consciousness in what had once
been the *SAO* server. That he'd spared me and Asuna, and left
something with me.

She looked at the ground for several minutes, shed a tear, and
said, "I visited his mountain retreat with the intent of killing him.
But I couldn't do it. And because of that, many young people lost
their lives. What he and I did cannot be forgiven. If you hate him,
please delete what he gave to you. But…if you do happen to feel
any emotion other than hatred…"

"Kirito. Hello, Kirito? About today's IRL meet-up…"

The elbow in my ribs brought me back to my senses.

"Oh—sorry. I was spacing out."

"No matter which world we're in, when you get lost in thought,
you really have no idea what's going on."

Asuna shook her head in exasperation, then unleashed a smile
like a ray of sunlight and plopped her head against my shoulder.

—∿∿—

With a most unladylike sound, I sucked the last remnants of
the strawberry yogurt drink through my straw. We were seated
against the west-facing cafeteria windows, at the third table
in—at least, as measured by the adjoining southern wall. Keiko
Ayano, who was sitting across from me, looked peeved.

"Can't you drink that any quieter, Liz—I mean, Rika?"

"Well, how else am I supposed to—oh geez, can you believe how close Kirito's sitting to her?"

A boy and girl were sitting shoulder to shoulder on the bench down in the courtyard, which was only visible through the tree branches from this exact table.

"Shameless. Right in the middle of school..."

"A-and you don't think it's rude to spy on them?!"

I gave Keiko a glance and remarked, "Remind me again who was just watching them very intently a moment ago, Silica?"

Silica the dagger wielder, also known as Keiko (or should that be the other way around?), went bright red and shoveled her shrimp pilaf into her mouth to avoid having to respond to that.

I crushed the empty drink pack and tossed it into the trash can several feet away, then rested my chin on my hands, sighing dramatically.

"Sheesh...If I'd known this would happen, I wouldn't have agreed to that one-month cease-fire."

"That was your idea, Liz! You said we should give them a month to enjoy their company...You should have known this would be the result."

"You have rice on your cheek."

I sighed again and stared up through the skylight at the clouds passing overhead.

Kirito had sent me an e-mail out of the blue in mid-February. I don't know how he got my address.

At first I was shocked, but then I heard the bell inside my head ring, signaling the start of round two. I headed to his meet-up spot, where he told me something even more shocking.

He'd gotten himself wrapped up in that shocking *ALO* Incident. And not only that, Asuna was a victim of it as well, though that was a secret from the public.

Asuna wanted to see me, so naturally, I rushed to visit her. When I saw how tender and fragile she looked, like a pale snow fairy, I felt that familiar urge to protect her that I'd experienced so many times in Aincrad.

Fortunately, she was getting better by day, and was able to start school along with the rest of us. Even once we were standing side by side again, I couldn't force myself to see her as a rival. She was still more of a little sister who needed my help, so another friend of mine who was in love with Kirito decided to form an alliance with me—the alliance to let them be lovebirds until the end of May. And yet…

I sighed for a third time and popped the last bite of BLT into my mouth, then looked to Silica. "Gonna go to the IRL meet-up?"

"Of course I am. Lea—Suguha is coming, too. I can't wait; I've never met her in person before."

"You've got quite a nice relationship with Leafa," I smirked at her. "Must be because you have so much in common, both being little-sister figures."

"Grr…"

She grimaced, chowed down the last of her pilaf, and returned the smirk.

"Well, Liz, I guess that makes you the older sister now."

Our glares sent sparks flying. A few moments later, we both looked up at the clouds and sighed together.

The ugly black door of Agil's Dicey Café was adorned with an ugly sign that said RESERVED in ugly handwriting.

I turned to Suguha and asked, "Have you ever met Agil, Sugu?"

"Yeah, we hunted together twice, I think. He was real big."

"He's just like that in real life, too, so get ready."

Suguha's eyes went wide. Beside her, Asuna giggled.

"I certainly was surprised the first time I visited."

"Me, too. I was freaked out."

I bopped Suguha's frightened head and gave her a grin before pushing the door open. The bell clanged briefly, but was drowned out by a sudden cheer of applause and whistling.

The small interior was already packed with people. The speakers were blaring some in-game BGM—surprisingly enough, the Algade theme song played by the NPC musicians in Aincrad—and glasses full of drinks shone in every hand. The party was well under way.

"What gives? We didn't show up late!" I protested, stunned. Lisbeth sidled up in her school uniform.

"Heh, the star of the show always has to be the last to arrive. We just told you it started at a later time than everyone else. C'mon in!"

She pulled the three of us inside and shoved us onto the little stage at the back of the café. The door slammed shut, the music died out, and the lights turned up.

Suddenly I was washed in the spotlight, and beyond the glare I heard Lisbeth say, "All right everyone, are we ready? One, two, three!"

"Congrats on beating *SAO*, Kirito!!" the entire room chanted. Party crackers popped. There was applause.

Picture flashes went off right in my dumbfounded face.

Today's offline meet-up, the "Aincrad Conquest Celebration," had been originally planned by me, Liz and Agil, but at some point the reins had been seized by everyone else *but* me. There was at least double the number of people inside the building as I'd expected.

After a toast, we had a round of introductions, followed by a speech from me—not planned or prepared for—and a number of Agil's massive homemade pizzas. The party was in complete chaos at this point.

The ways I was congratulated individually were varied—raucous and hearty from the men, a little *too* intimate from the women, and by the time I got to one of the stools at the bar counter, I was exhausted.

"Bourbon on the rocks, boss," I ordered glibly. The large man in the white shirt and black necktie gave me an appraising look.

A few moments later, to my surprise, a tumbler came sliding over with ice cubes and an amber liquid inside.

I took a tiny, hesitant sip to find that it was nothing more than oolong tea. I sneered back at the bartender, who was very pleased with himself. Meanwhile, a tall, skinny fellow plopped onto the stool next to me. He was dressed in a suit with an ugly tie, and stunningly enough, an even uglier bandanna.

"The real thing for me, Agil."

It was Klein, the katana warrior. Glass in hand, he swiveled around on the stool to cast a leering glance at a group of women chattering happily across the room.

"Really, drinks in the afternoon? Aren't you going to work after this?"

"Bah. Who can stomach overtime without a drink or two in 'em? Besides...hot damn..."

He continued staring goonishly at the girls. I rolled my eyes and tossed back a mouthful of iced tea.

I had to admit, it was a pretty nice sight. Asuna, Lisbeth, Silica, Sasha, Yuriel, and Suguha, together at once—it made me want to take a picture. As a matter of fact, the entire thing was being videotaped...for Yui's sake.

Another man took the other adjacent stool. He was in a suit himself, but unlike Klein, he looked the part of a proper businessman. This was Thinker, the former commander of the Army.

I raised my glass and said to him, "I hear you tied the knot with Yuriel? A bit belated, but—congrats." We clinked glasses, and he laughed shyly.

"Well, I've just been trying my hardest to get used to real life again. Work's finally on the right track, too..."

Klein raised his drink as well and leaned in. "Seriously, cheers! I shoulda found someone for myself while I was there. By the way, I've been checking out the new MMO today."

Thinker smiled shyly again. "Aw, geez. We barely have anything up on the site yet... Besides, strategy data and MMO news are quickly becoming obsolete."

"The birth of a new universe is a time of chaos," I nodded, then looked at the bartender, who was rattling a shaker. "How's The Seed been since then, Agil?"

The bald man put on a toothy smile that would make a small child cry and chortled, "It's incredible. We've got about fifty mirrors up, downloads in six figures now, and nearly three hundred functioning servers running."

Akihiko Kayaba's thought-simulation program had left me the "seed of a world."

A few days after meeting with his former assistant, I had Yui transfer the massive file from my NerveGear's local storage to a memory chip, and brought it to Agil's bar. He was the only person I knew with the skills to help that seed take root.

Naturally, there was hatred within me for Kayaba and his floating castle world. His game of death killed several people I thought of as friends. It was for their sake, for the memory of their terror, as well as my girlfriend, that I could never forgive Kayaba for what he did.

But unfortunately, I couldn't deny that somewhere within that great loathing, there was an ounce of empathy for him. With true life and death, he had created another reality. I was desperate to escape that world, but I also loved it. Somewhere deep within my heart, a part of me was constantly hoping for it to continue.

After much hard thought, I came to a conclusion: I wanted to see what would grow from this "seed."

The seed of a world.

It was a program package designed by Kayaba, officially titled "The Seed," that contained everything necessary for a full-sensory VR full-dive system.

Not only had he downsized the Cardinal system—which controlled and managed the *SAO* server—into a compact size that even a small server could run, he'd even packed in the development suite necessary for all the software game components.

In other words, anyone who wanted to create their own VR world, as long as they had a server with a good enough connection, could download the package, design 3D objects or utilize others' creations, and run the program to create their own world.

Developing a program that managed the input and output for all five senses was incredibly difficult. In essence, every VR game in the entire world was based on some form of Kayaba's Cardinal system, at incredible licensing cost.

With the end of Argus, control of the program transferred to RCT, and with the end of RCT Progress, a new buyer was needed. But the cost of the software and the social stigma of the VR genre were enough to drive off any company rich enough to afford it. To most observers, the genre was bound to die off.

Into that void stepped The Seed, a compact VR control system that was entirely rights free. I gave the program to Agil, who used his connections to analyze the program thoroughly and determine that it did not pose any harm.

Whether Kayaba's intended it to be harmless or not, ultimately no one other than its creator could foresee what might happen if this software was unleashed upon the world. Yet I couldn't help but feel that a very simple emotion was at the heart of his plan.

The desire to see a true "other world."

At my request, Agil uploaded The Seed to servers all over the world, so that anyone, individual or company, could access it.

Ultimately, *ALfheim Online* was saved from an untimely demise by a number of venture capitalists who were also *ALO* players. They banded together to form a new company, and managed to acquire all of the *ALO* data from RCT at a rock-bottom price.

Alfheim's vast continent was brought back to life within a new crucible with all player data intact. Apparently, not even 10 percent of the player base had given up the game for good after the incident.

Of course, Alfheim was not the only world brought to life. From companies without the funds to afford the astronomical licensing fee down to single individuals, hundreds of new developers appeared, running their own VR game servers. Some charged fees and some didn't. These games gradually found themselves aligning and connecting to one another, leading to the formation of some meta-rules widely accepted across the spectrum. There was even a common agreement that a character created in one VR game should be easily convertible across *all* game worlds.

The Seed's functionality didn't stop merely at games. Education, communication, tourism—servers offering new experiences popped up by the day, giving birth to an ever-greater variety of worlds. The day was coming soon when the total size of combined VR worlds eclipsed the land area of Japan itself.

Thinker smiled and spoke with dreamy eyes.

"I honestly think we're witnessing the birth of a new world. The term *MMORPG* is too narrow to describe it. I actually want to come up with a new name for my website...but nothing good comes to mind."

"Hmmm," Klein murmured, crossing his arms and furrowing his brow in thought. I jabbed his elbow and laughed.

"Come on, nobody's looking for suggestions from a guy who'd name his guild Furinkazan!"

"What? We're fast as the wind, still as the forest, fierce as fire, and immovable as the mountain! People are lining up for days to join the new Furinkazan!"

"Good for you. Hopefully you can recruit some cute girls."

"Ugh..."

Klein had no response to that. I laughed again and turned back to Agil. "There are no changes to the after-party plan, right?"

"Correct. We're meeting up at Yggdrasil City at eleven tonight."

"And," I lowered my voice, "is it going to work?"

"You bet. Took an entire new cloud of servers, but that's the legendary castle for ya. We've got more and more players signed up, and the funds are pouring in."

"Well, let's cross our fingers."

The former *SAO* server was reformatted and scrapped entirely. But among the former Argus materials the new *ALO* admins bought was something completely unexpected.

I drained my glass of tea and held it in both hands, looking at the ceiling of the bar. The black panels looked like night sky to me. Gray clouds floated past. Next the moon appeared, casting its blue glow on the world. Beyond that was a gigantic—

"Hey, Kirito! Over here!" Lisbeth bellowed, fully drunk now. She waved me over dramatically.

"I hope she's not too hammered," I said, eyeing the large pitcher full of pink liquid in her hands. The outlaw bartender played it cool.

"Don't worry, it's only one percent alcohol. Besides, tomorrow's the weekend."

"Oh, come on…"

I stood up, shaking my head. It was going to be a long evening.

———

Leafa flew through the pitch-black night.

Her two pairs of wings beat against the air, propelling her onward, faster and faster. The wind screamed in her ears.

Before, she'd had to master the art of gliding to conserve her limited wing power, finding just the right combination of cruising speed and swooping trajectory. But that was all in the past now. There were no more shackles imposed upon her by the system.

There was no city on top of the World Tree after all. The alfs, fairies of light, did not exist. The King of the Fairies, who was said to transform anyone who could reach him, was a false tyrant.

But now that the land had fallen into ruin and been brought back by a new ruler—or managers—every fairy in the game was given eternal wings. She was still a green wind sylph, not an alf, but Leafa was happy as she was.

She logged in a full hour before the time of the meeting and left the cait sith stronghold of Freelia, which had been her home base recently. She'd been flying for twenty minutes straight, not resting for a second but buzzing her wings at full power, indulging her impulses. Despite such a long flight at top speed, her grass-green propellers never lost an ounce of power. They stayed faithful to Leafa's commands through thick and thin.

Kirito had described the acceleration theory under the new order of Alfheim as an automobile. Just after leaving the ground, you had to spread your wings as wide as possible "for the purposes of torque"—Kirito's words, whatever that meant—and catch as much air as you could in each beat.

Once the speed was up to a good level, the wings should be bent at a tight angle and beat quick and short. Once at maximum speed, you could fold the wings into a straight line, vibrating them so fast they were virtually invisible. From the ground, a player at that speed was nothing but a colorful comet. At that point, there was very little that could be done to increase speed; it depended entirely on the flyer's will and guts. Most would slow down from either instinctual fear or mental exhaustion.

Last week they'd held a race across Alfheim, which was highlighted by a dead heat between Leafa and Kirito that she won by a hair at the very end. They demolished the competition so badly that the prospect of a second race was unlikely at this point.

That was so much fun…

Leafa chuckled to herself as she flew. Kirito trailed her as they approached the goal line, and he'd tried the underhanded tactic of telling stupid jokes in an attempt to make her laugh and lose concentration. It had worked like gangbusters. If she hadn't hit him perfectly with the antidote potion in her pouch, he might well have overtaken her.

Racing like that was fun, but there was nothing like letting her mind empty as she sped away toward the horizon on her own.

Her long flight had brought her very close to the maximum speed. The dark land below was only a striped blur to her eyes, and any lights from the small towns she saw ahead were behind her in moments.

Just when she physically felt like she was going faster than she'd ever flown before, Leafa spread her wings and twisted into a steep climb.

A full moon was shining through a crack in the thick clouds above. She rose like a rocket, heading straight for the pale disc. A few seconds later, she plunged into the clouds, noting a slight difference in the sound in her ears. She pierced the black veil like a bullet. A bolt of lightning flashed very close by, illuminating the clouds around her, but she did not stop.

Finally she broke through. The entire world was lit by pale blue moonlight—the surface below was an unbroken field of white clouds. The only other object in sight was the top of the World Tree in the distance, towering over the cloud layer. Her speed was indeed dropping by now, but Leafa only tensed her lips and straightened out her fingers, reaching for that moon. It seemed to her that the silver platter was getting larger and larger. She could make out the individual craters.

Was it just a trick of the eyes that made her think she saw a group of glinting lights in the center of one of the larger craters? Could there be an unknown civilization up on that moon, living in a town of their own? If she could just get a bit closer...

But eventually Leafa was caught by the end of the world, the game's altitude limit. Her speed dropped abruptly and her body grew heavy. The virtual world ended right ahead. It just wasn't possible to go any farther. But...

Leafa reached out as far as she could, spreading her fingers as though to grab the moon.

I want to go there. Higher. Farther. Out of the stratosphere, free from gravity, to that moon world. And beyond that, too—between the planets, surpassing the comets, out into the ocean of stars...

Her upward acceleration finally died and went negative. Leafa went into a free fall in the night sky, her arms held wide. Bit by bit, the moon grew smaller.

Leafa closed her eyes and smiled.

Maybe not yet, but soon…

According to Kirito, *ALfheim Online* was in the planning stages to join a vast VRMMO nexus. They'd start by interfacing with a game set on the surface of the moon. Once that happened, she'd be able to fly there. Eventually others would join and take their places as planets, and interstellar ferries would be able to take her through the cosmos.

I can fly anywhere. I can go anywhere… except for one place.

The thought suddenly made her sad. She hugged herself tight as she fell toward the fluffy cloud layer.

She knew why she felt lonely. It was because of the party she'd attended in the real world with Kirito—her brother, Kazuto.

It was so much fun. She'd been able to meet many of his friends in person for the first time, to talk face-to-face. Those three hours had passed in a blink.

But at the same time, she felt the existence of a bond that tied them all together, something invisible but powerful: the memories of their shared battles, tears, laughs, and love from the floating castle of Aincrad. Even now, back in the real world, these things shone brightly within them.

Her love for Kazuto had not changed.

She felt the same sensation of warm sunlight when she said good night in his doorway, or ran to the station with him in the morning.

If they'd been true siblings, or total strangers growing up in different cities, she might have shed bitter tears. But she was lucky: She got to spend every day living with him under the same roof. She didn't need his entire heart. As long as there was a tiny bit of space in there for her, that was enough.

I've finally gotten myself to be content with that.

But at that party, she'd felt a premonition that Kazuto would one day travel far away, far beyond her reach. She couldn't intrude into that bond that group shared. There was no place for Suguha there; she held no memories of that castle.

Leafa curled into a ball and dropped like a meteor.

The clouds were very close. The meeting place was in the new Yggdrasil City, built into the top of the World Tree. She needed to spread her wings and begin gliding soon. But the coldness sealing her heart prevented her from doing so.

The cold wind brushed her cheek, stealing the warmth from her breast. She sank deeper, deeper into the dark sea of clouds...

Suddenly, something caught her, stopping her fall.

"___?!"

Leafa's eyes shot open in surprise.

There was Kirito's face, right in front of her. He was holding her in his arms, hovering just above the clouds. Before she could ask why, the tanned spriggan spoke.

"I was wondering how far you'd go. C'mon, the meeting's just about to start."

"...Oh...Thanks."

Leafa smiled, beat her wings, and rolled out of his arms.

The management operating the new *ALfheim Online* received the entire collection of game data from RCT Progress, which included within it the old character data from *Sword Art Online*. The operators decided that when former *SAO* players started an account in the new *ALO*, they could choose to carry over their old character and appearance from *SAO* if they wished.

Therefore, Leafa's regular partners—Silica, Asuna, Lisbeth—were extremely close to their original appearance, just with a few fairylike features added. But when Kirito was given the choice, he decided to stick with his spriggan form, rather than return to his old look. He also reset his phenomenal statistics so that he could start over from the beginning.

Leafa was struck with a sudden urge to know why, so she asked Kirito as they hovered side by side.

"Hey, Big Br...Kirito, why didn't you go back to your old look like the others?"

"Hmm..."

He folded his arms and looked hazily into the distance, and then grinned.

"The Kirito from that world finished his quest."

"...I see," she laughed.

The thought that she was the one who had first happened across Kirito the spriggan and helped him travel to the World Tree filled her with a kind of pride. She floated over and took his hand.

"Let's dance."

"Huh?"

His eyes went wide. She tugged at his arm and slid over the top of the clouds.

"It's an advanced technique just recently developed. You can move around sideways while maintaining a hover."

"Ohh..."

That seemed to have stimulated his desire for a good challenge. He attempted to mimic her movements, his face locked in concentration. But he soon tipped forward and lost his balance.

"Nwah!"

"Hee-hee! It won't work if you try to accelerate forward. It's more like the teensiest bit of lift, plus a glide to the side."

"Hrrm..."

Leafa pulled him by the arm, and after a few minutes of awkward stumbling, Kirito seemed to have gotten the hang of it.

"Oh...I see, like this?"

"That's it. You're doing good!"

Leafa smiled and took a small bottle from her waist pocket. She pulled out the cork and let it float in midair. Little dots of silver light flooded out of the bottle, along with the sound of a beautiful string ensemble. It was a musical item sold by high-level pooka minstrels, a recording of one of their performances.

Leafa began to step gracefully to the rhythm.

Big step, little step, big again, they floated through the air. She stared into Kirito's eyes as they held hands, helping him decide which direction to turn in the moment.

They spun and spun across the endless ocean of clouds, lit by pale moonlight. Their slow, graceful actions gradually went faster, farther, with each step of the dance.

The green light scattered by Leafa's wings and the white light of Kirito's mingled in the air and vanished. The sound of the wind faded away. She shut her eyes.

She could feel all of Kirito's emotions and sentiments through his fingertips. This could be the last time for that. It was another one of those rare but magical moments where their hearts made direct contact. This would probably be the last of those.

Kirito—Kazuto—had his own world. School, friends, and those even closer. His wings were so strong, his stride so long, that she would never be able to reach him.

Their paths had been going in different directions ever since the day two years ago that he'd left for that other world and hadn't come back. She'd found this pair of fairy wings in the hopes that they would bring her closer, but half of the hearts of Kirito and the others were still within that floating castle of fantasy.

Scientific progress had made the world of the imagination impossibly real. It had surpassed the construct of a simple "game" and made the virtual into reality. But people are not built to live in many realities. Kazuto had experienced too much joy, sadness, and love in that other world. The world of dreams, a place Suguha herself would never visit.

She felt tears squeezing through her shut eyelids.

"Leafa…?" Kirito said into her ear.

She opened her eyes and looked at his smiling face. The music coming from the little bottle faded out, and the bottle itself quietly shattered into nothing.

"I'm going to go back home for today," she said, letting go of his hands.

"Huh? Why…?"

"Because…" She felt the tears return. "It's just…too far away from me. The place where you and everyone else are. I can't reach you there."

"Sugu…" He stared at her solemnly, then shook his head. "That's not true. You can go anywhere if you set your mind to it."

He took her hand without waiting for an answer, squeezed it, and turned away.

"Ah…"

Kirito beat his wings powerfully and began to accelerate. He headed straight for the World Tree, across the sea of clouds.

Kirito raced along at ferocious speed, not easing his grip on Leafa's hand an ounce. She struggled to keep up so that she wouldn't be dragged along.

In time, the World Tree grew large enough to cover their view of the sky. At the top of the trunk, where the first massive limbs branched out, there was a gathering of countless tiny lights: Yggdrasil City.

Kirito flew toward a tower in the center that stood taller and brighter than the others. Just as they got close enough to discern between the lights beyond open windows and the lights hanging from streetlamps, a great pealing of many bells sounded.

It was Alfheim's signal for midnight. The sound emitted from the great hollow space within the trunk of the tree, wherein an elevator between Alne and Yggdrasil City had been installed. From there, the sound traveled across the entire world.

Kirito spread his wings to come to an abrupt stop.

"Whoa—!" Leafa wasn't quick enough to react, and she would have collided with him if he hadn't stretched out his arms to snag her.

"We didn't make it in time. Here it comes."

"Huh?"

She looked at him, uncomprehending. Kirito smiled and winked, pointing to a stretch of sky above. She turned around in his arms and looked up at the night sky.

The gigantic full moon was glowing with a cold blue light. But that was all.

"Um… it's the moon. What about it?"

"Look closer." He gestured higher. She squinted.

Along the upper right curve of the silver circle, a tiny piece was missing.

"Huh...?"

She looked harder. An eclipse? But nothing like that had ever happened in Alfheim, to her knowledge.

The black shadow stealing over the moon grew and grew. But the shape itself was not a circle. It was like a triangular wedge, digging farther and farther into the sphere. A low growl hit Leafa's ears. Something was echoing heavily—*gong, gong.* It shook the entire atmosphere, as if emanating from a great distance.

The shadow was now blocking out the moon entirely. But the moon's light, wrapping around, did still dimly illuminate the contours of the triangular shadow. Larger it grew. Larger, and closer—

It was a conical object, but the distance to it was hard to grasp. Leafa squinted for a better look.

The floating object suddenly lit up on its own. Bright beams of yellow light sprayed in all directions.

It seemed to be made of a great many thin layers that were stacked on top of each other, and the light was streaming from between the layers. Three massive pillars hung from the bottom of the object, ending in points that glowed on their own.

A ship? A house? Leafa couldn't tell. Meanwhile, the thing only got more gargantuan. It was completely blocking out an entire part of the sky. The heavy rumbling vibrated her body.

Suddenly, she realized that she could see something between the bottom two layers. Tiny little fixtures sprouting up and down. In fact, they looked like...

Buildings! There were a number of massive buildings with several floors' worth of windows. But based on the size of the building, each one of the dozens of layers had to be at least as tall as the Tower of Wind. In that case, how tall must the entire structure be? How many hundreds and hundreds of feet? How many miles...?

"Ah…that—that can't be…" A shocking thought shot through Leafa's brain. "Is that…?"

She turned and looked at Kirito. He nodded gravely, but couldn't keep the excitement from his voice.

"That's right. It's Aincrad, the floating castle."

"But…why? Why is it here…?"

The floating structure slowed its approach, and stopped when it was nearly close enough to touch the highest branches of the World Tree.

"So we can finish what we started," he replied softly. "We'll beat it from the first floor to the hundredth this time. I only got three-quarters of the way through last time. Leafa…"

He let his hand rest on top of her head. "I'm a lot weaker than I used to be…You'll help me, won't you?"

"…Ah…"

The word caught in her throat. She stared at him.

You can go anywhere if you set your mind to it.

Tears fell down her cheeks again, falling to Kirito's shirt.

"Yeah. I'll be with you…together…wherever you go…"

A voice floated up to them from below as they gazed at the impossibly large castle.

"Hey! You're late, Kirito!"

Leafa looked back to see Klein rising to meet them, a yellow-and-black bandanna pushing up his red hair and a wildly long katana at his side.

Next to him was Agil with his massive battle-ax, his brown skin the mark of a gnome.

Lisbeth, with her white-and-blue apron, and a silver leprechaun hammer.

Silica, with luscious black ears and tail, a little blue dragon on her shoulder.

Sasha, who was not yet used to flying, wobbling along with her flight stick.

Sakuya and Alicia Rue, with their own contingent of sylphs and cait siths.

Recon, waving wildly.

Even Eugene the salamander and some of his men.

"C'mon, we're gonna leave you in the dust!" Klein shouted, and the entire ensemble raced off through the night, heading for the castle in the sky.

Last of all, dressed in a white tunic and miniskirt with a silver rapier at her side, stood Asuna, a tiny pixie on her shoulder. She stopped in front of Leafa and Kirito, her long hair waving.

"Let's go, Leafa!" Asuna urged, extending a hand. Leafa took it hesitantly. Asuna smiled and turned, beating her pale blue wings.

Yui hopped off of her shoulder and landed on Kirito's. "Hurry up, Papa!"

Kirito gave Aincrad a brief but serene gaze before hanging his head. His lips moved, as though saying someone's name to himself, but his voice was inaudible.

When he looked up again, Kirito was wearing his usual invincible smile. He spread his wings and pointed up to the heavens.

"All right—let's go!!"

(The End)

AFTERWORD

Hello, this is Reki Kawahara. Thank you for picking up *Sword Art Online 4: Fairy Dance*, my eighth published book.

This two-volume story was both a continuation of the story from Volume 1, and a very, very long epilogue. At the time I started writing it, I was only planning on having it be about the hero, Kirito, searching for and finding the heroine, Asuna. But the more I added to the story, the longer it grew in the telling.

One of those features I tried to explore was the question, "Can you write a novel just about playing a normal RPG?"

At the time I wrote *SAO* Volume 1, I thought that an RPG story required something extra to work as a proper novel. After all, no matter the terrible odds the hero faces in a game, the person controlling him in real life doesn't suffer a single scratch. In order to sidestep the dual issues of "it's just a game" and "you can start over at any time," I came up with the concept of the game of death: Dying within the game means dying in real life.

But there was a part of me that wondered if this was really true. If an RPG novel isn't worth it without a catch like that, then what does that say about all the thrills and chills I've experienced playing MMOs? Were they false emotions? I wanted to try evoking the excitement and fun I had when my friends and I formed a party and challenged our first dungeon. That ended up being a large creative theme within *Fairy Dance*.

I suppose you'll know whether I succeeded or not if, having

just turned the final page, you feel like trying out an MMO right now (ha-ha).

The very straightforward "virtual-reality online game" *SAO* series is going to take a big shift in the next volume, whether that ends up being ill-advised or just plain chaotic. Those readers who enjoyed the taste of the original story might be extremely confused, but I assure you that Kirito will continue to be the unchanging core of the series, so I hope you'll continue to partake in his adventures.

Once again, great thanks must go out to Abec for her delicate illustrations of all the new characters and monsters, and to my editor, Mr. Miki, for putting up with my terribly late submissions! And all the rest of the gratitude remaining in my hard drive goes out to you for reading this!

Reki Kawahara—January 28, 2010

HOW FANTASY SPORTS
EXPLAINS THE WORLD